INVASION OF THE TIME TROOPERS

D0068334

TIMEBENDERS

#1. *Battle Before Time*

#2. *Doorway to Doom*

#3. *Invasion of the Time Troopers*

#4. *Lost in Cydonia*

Visit the author, Jim Denney, at
www.denneybooks.com/timebenders.html.

TIMEBENDERS

INVASION OF THE TIME TROOPERS

JIM DENNEY

Tommy
NELSON®

www.tommynelson.com

A Division of Thomas Nelson, Inc.
www.ThomasNelson.com

INVASION OF THE TIME TROOPERS

Text copyright © 2002 Jim Denney

Published in Nashville, Tennessee, by Tommy Nelson®, a Division of Thomas Nelson, Inc.

Library of Congress Cataloging-in-Publication Data

Denney, James D.
    Invasion of the Time Troopers / Jim Denney.
        p. cm. — (Timebenders ; #3)
    Summary: When Max is hijacked fifty years into the future and faces the evil of witchcraft, his friends have their own adventures while trying to rescue him.
    ISBN 140030041X
    [1. Christian life—Fiction. 2. Time travel—Fiction. 3. Witchcraft—Fiction.] 1. Title.

PZ7.D4272 In 2002
[Fic] 21   2002029536

Printed in the United States of America

02 03 04 05 06 PHX 5 4 3 2 1

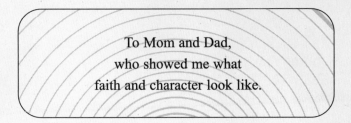

To Mom and Dad,
who showed me what
faith and character look like.

Contents

1

THE IMPOSSIBLE THING THAT HAPPENED

Max McCrane's time machine sat in the middle of his backyard. The time machine looked like an ordinary old, orange Volkswagen Beetle. Max had spent the summer working on the car, pounding out dents, scrubbing dried swamp mud off the floorboards, and shining up the chrome bumper. Then he invited Allie O'Dell and Grady Stubblefield to come see the result.

Allie and Grady weren't just Max's best friends at Victor Appleton Middle School. They were also fellow time travelers with Max on two previous adventures. When Allie and Grady arrived at Max's big Victorian house on Mirabilis Way, he led them around to the backyard.

Allie ran up and touched the smooth, shiny fender of the VW. "It's beautiful!" she said. "It almost looks like new!"

The autumn sun sparkled in her braces and made her carrot-red ponytail shine as if it were on fire.

"My dad helped me pound out the dents," Max said. "And my mom helped me patch up the dashboard and seat covers." His brown eyes gleamed with pride behind the large, round lenses of his glasses, and a breeze ruffled his unruly brown hair. He wore a gray sweatshirt, black pants, and gray Nike running shoes.

"You replaced all the broken glass," Grady said, walking around the car. He was an African-American with an athletic build, short hair, and a ready grin. "New paint job, too—but why *orange?*"

Max shrugged. "Why *not* orange? It was orange before." He opened the door and sat down behind the wheel.

"Yeah," Grady said, "but if you're going to repaint it, why paint it the same ugly color? Why not cherry red or midnight blue?"

"Because," Max said, "this is Timebender. We had two awesome adventures in this old car. If I painted Timebender some other color it would have been like—well, like it wasn't really Timebender anymore." Max reached over to the glove box and flipped on the power switch, then he picked up the computer keyboard that was Timebender's control panel.

"What are you doing?" Allie asked.

Max tapped a couple of keys on the keyboard. "Just a battery check and a memory reset," he said. "I check it every once in a while, just to make sure everything's— Hey, Grady, are you okay?"

"Look at that!" Grady said. He was staring at an orange shimmer in the air over the lawn.

Max jumped out of the car and joined his two friends. All three of them stared at the orange shimmer.

It took shape and solidified into an orange VW Beetle like Timebender. But *this* VW Beetle was different from Timebender in several important ways. For one thing, this VW was dented and bashed, and its windows were cracked and broken. The driver's-side door was missing. Someone had painted bright, colorful designs on the car: rainbows, butterflies, white doves, and flowers—lots and lots of flowers. Along the rear fender, the words FLOWER POWER appeared in bright blue paint.

There were three people in the flowered VW, and they all came tumbling out. The first one came from the driver's side, where the door was missing. She was a red-haired girl with braces. When Allie saw the girl, she gave a shriek. She was looking at *herself!*

The second one out of the car was a lean, athletic-looking African-American with short hair. Grady's jaw dropped. "You," he said, pointing to the black youth. "You're me! I mean, I'm you! I mean—What's happening?"

Max looked back and forth, from Allie to Allie, from Grady to Grady. Both Allies were dressed exactly alike— denim overalls, pink top, pink scrunchie, white tennis shoes. Both girls had the same freckles, the same braces on their teeth, and the same carrot-red ponytail. It was as if the two Allies were identical twins.

Both Gradys were also dressed exactly alike: baggy blue jeans, a black Tommy Hilfiger shirt, and black Lugz sneakers. With a sense of fear, Max was sure he knew who would emerge next: another Max McCrane.

The third person pushed his way from the backseat of the Volkswagen, tripped on his way out, and went sprawling onto the grass. Max's eyes widened. The third person out of the flowered VW was not Max. It was—

"Toby!" Max said in astonishment. "Toby Brubaker!"

Toby scrambled to his feet. He was a thickset boy, built like a fireplug, with bristly, close-cropped hair, doughy skin, a pug nose, and beady, pale-green eyes. There were pink smears on his face and arms, and his clothes were dirty and grass-stained. Toby Brubaker was no friend of Max, Allie, or Grady—he had caused them nothing but trouble on their two previous trips in time.

As Max, Allie, and Grady stared in astonishment, the other Allie, Grady, and the wide-eyed Toby began shouting and gesturing all at once. They were trying to say something, but it was all a meaningless babble because everybody was yelling at once.

Max, Allie, and Grady stared in shock. They thought this was the most impossible thing that could happen. But in the next instant, something even more impossible happened.

Just a few yards behind the flowered Volkswagen, another shimmer appeared. The shimmer solidified into a strange black-and-white vehicle—a hovercar that floated two feet off the ground. It had a transparent bubble canopy on top. The words TIME TROOPERS were printed on the side of the hovercar in gold letters.

"They found us!" the other Allie screamed.

"Let's get out of here!" the other Grady shouted.

"Aaaaggghhh!" Toby wailed.

The trio jumped back into the flowered VW—Allie in the driver's seat, Grady in the passenger seat, and Toby in back.

Doors opened out of both sides of the black-and-white hovercar. Ramps were lowered to the grass. Men in black-and-white metal armor and helmets walked down the ramps, carrying pistol-shaped devices in their hands. The pistol devices had crystal lenses in front and reminded Max of laser blasters in a sci-fi movie.

As the armored men stepped onto the grass, Max realized they weren't *men* at all. What at first appeared to be metal armor was actually metal *skin*. The black-and-white metal "men" were actually *robots*.

Each robot had a face of molded steel. Where the eyes should have been were glass disks, like camera lenses. Behind those lenses, pinpricks of cold blue light burned. Where the mouth should have been was a black metal disk, like a radio speaker. Max noticed that each robot had gold lettering on its black-metal chest. On one robot was written: TIME TROOPER 7; on the other: TIME TROOPER 11.

The robots approached the flowered VW, pointing their pistol devices at the three people inside. "Halt!" one of them said in a flat, electronic voice. "Do not engage your time circuits!"

But before the robot had finished speaking, the flowered VW winked out of existence!

"This," said one of the robots, "is getting to be a habit."

The two robots ran back to their hovercar and dashed up the ramps. The doors swung shut. Seconds later, the hovercar winked out of existence.

"What just happened?" Allie asked in a frightened whisper. "Did I just see—me?"

"Yeah," Grady said. "One of them was you, and one of them was me."

"But where was I?" Max asked. "How come there wasn't another me in that car? And why was Toby there?"

"Guys," Allie said, "I am sooo freaked!"

"Dude!" said a voice behind them. They all jumped. They knew that voice—the voice of Toby Brubaker, the voice of trouble. They turned and saw Toby approaching— and a girl was with him.

"Oh, no!" Allie groaned. "Toby—and Luna Skyes!"

Toby was dressed like the Toby they had seen just moments before—a white tee shirt and cargo pants. But *this* Toby had no pink smears on his skin and face, and his clothes were clean and neat, not grass-stained and dirty. Oddly, he wore a backpack—an empty one, judging from its flat and saggy appearance.

Luna's hair, which was somewhere between gold and platinum in color, contrasted sharply with her clothes— designer blue jeans, purple designer top, purple dangles, purple hoop bracelets, a purple purse, and even purple lip gloss. It was all a bit too much—but then, so was Luna.

"Guys," Max hissed, "not a word to them about what just happened!"

"Right," Grady whispered back.

"Not a word," Allie said.

"You people look like you've seen a ghost!" Luna said as she walked toward them.

Max groped for words. "We're, uh, kind of surprised to see you," he said. "I mean, you and Toby don't usually come here. What's up?"

Luna glanced at Toby. "Toby and I were talking about those time trips you guys took on Time Blender—"

"It's Time*bender*, Luna," Max corrected. "It's a machine that bends time."

"Whatever," Luna said. "The thing is, I knew you guys had seen, like, dinosaurs and stuff. But Toby was telling me something I'd never heard before. He said you saw some kind of spirit beings—Emissaries, I think he called them."

"That's right," Max said.

"Well," Luna said, "you know that I'm into all kinds of

spiritual stuff—astrology, tarot cards, Ouija boards, spells, and incantations. I'm not religious, but I'm *very* spiritual."

"Tarot cards? Ouija boards?" Allie said. "That's not spiritual, Luna. That's just stupid. You shouldn't mess with the occult."

Toby's eyes narrowed. "What kind of cult?"

"Not a *cult*, Toby," Allie said. "The *occult*. You know— the supernatural, witchcraft, astrology? Some of it's just nonsense and superstition, but some of it involves real evil powers, and it's dangerous to your soul."

Luna laughed. "'Dangerous to your soul'!" she said while shaking her head. "Allie, dear, that shows how little you understand. Fortunately for you, I've decided to be the bigger person and show tolerance toward your narrow-minded attitude. But getting back to the reason I came—"

"Yeah, Luna," Toby said. "Tell them."

"I want to go back in time," Luna said.

Max gulped. "But, Luna—"

"Oh, look!" Luna said. She walked past Max and admired her reflection in the shiny orange paint job of the Volkswagen Beetle. "New paint, new glass, no dents— nice job, Max! It looks much better."

"Yeah," Max said, "I spent the summer fixing it up."

Luna grabbed the handle, opened the driver's-side door, and sniffed inside. "Cool!" she said. "That yucky smell is gone. When you showed it to me before, it really reeked!"

"I know," Max said. "I used a whole can of Lysol."

"So," Luna said, turning around, "when can I go?"

"Wait a minute!" Max said. "We can't just get in and zoom off into the past!"

"But that's not fair!" Luna pouted. "You guys got to see real dinosaurs!"

"Yeah," Allie said, "and we almost got eaten."

"Dude!" Toby said. "What is this—some kind of exclusive club?"

"Look, Toby," Grady said, "after our first trip we offered to let you join us, remember? But you called us a bunch of losers and walked off."

Toby shrugged. "So I changed my mind. I want to be a Timebender now—and so does Luna. Are you going to let us join or what?"

Max, Allie, and Grady exchanged glances.

"Guys," Allie said, "let's go over there and talk it over." Max, Allie, and Grady walked to the far side of the car.

"Toby's up to something," Grady whispered. "I can smell it."

"Yeah," Allie agreed. "Luna, too. She's always scheming about something."

"Aren't you guys forgetting something?" Max said. "We've got a bigger problem. We have to find out why that other Volkswagen popped into my backyard, along with an Allie-twin, a Grady-twin, and a Toby-twin." He gulped, and his voice shook as he added, "And why there was no Max-twin."

"Yeah," Allie said. "I don't know which is scarier—that Grady and I saw our own doubles, or that you didn't."

"The thing I want to know," Grady said, "is why were we—they—our doubles being chased by robots?"

"Right," Allie said. "So what should we do about Toby and Luna?"

"Let's tell them they're official Timebenders," Max said. "Then let's get them out of my backyard so we can concentrate on the bigger problem."

"I agree," Grady said.

"Dude!" Toby shouted from the middle of the yard. "What's taking you dorks so long?"

Max, Allie, and Grady returned.

"What did you decide?" Luna asked with a toss of her ultrablond hair.

"Okay," Max said. "You're Timebenders—in your case, Luna, an honorary Timebender."

"Honorary, Max?" Luna asked. "Why not make it official? I'm ready to leave right now."

Allie looked at Max and shook her head.

Max shrugged. "Okay," he said. "I'll give you a time trip—but next week, okay?"

"No," Luna replied. "I'm ready *now*."

Allie muttered, "She's so pushy!"

Luna turned to Allie. "What did you say, Allie?"

Allie reddened. "Uh—the seats in the VW aren't very cushy."

Luna smirked. "They look comfortable enough to me. Well, Max?"

"Okay," Max said. "One quick trip. Who else wants to go?"

Before anyone could speak, Luna grabbed Max's arm and pulled him toward Timebender. "I think it should be just you and me, Max," she said. "The others had their turn, but this is my first trip."

"But Luna," Toby whined, "what about me? You said—"

"Next time, Toby," Luna said. "I want this trip to be just me and Max."

Allie groaned and rolled her eyes.

Max opened the passenger door for Luna, then he got in on the driver's side and slid behind the steering wheel.

Allie stood with her arms folded and her mouth smooshed to one side of her face. "This is *such* a bad idea!" she muttered.

"Where are you guys going?" asked Grady. "And how long will you be gone?"

Max rolled down the window. "I'll go to any time Luna wants to visit, as long as it's safe—no dinosaurs. And we'll be back in five minutes."

Luna didn't hesitate. "I know right where I want to go," she said. "October 31, 1939."

Max gave her a surprised look. "Why that exact date?"

Luna grinned smugly. "You'll see when we get there."

Max shrugged. "Okay," he said. He checked the batteries

in the glove box to make sure there was plenty of power. He took the computer keyboard from between the seats and laid it across his lap. Then he took out a spiral-bound notebook, a pencil, and a pocket calculator and made his calculations.

Luna looked bored. "Can't you just type in the date and go?"

"It's not that simple," Max said. "Time travel is a matter of physics and mathematics. If I make a mistake in these calculations, we could end up who-knows-when."

Luna sighed. "All right," she said. "Oh, and could you fix it so we'll arrive in the evening at, say, fivish?"

"Well," Max said, "I'll figure it as close as I can—but with time travel, it's hard to be exact. You have to allow for a few hours' error, plus or minus. I'll shoot for, uh, 'fivish'— but we could arrive anywhere from about 'twoish' to 'eightish.'"

Luna shrugged. "Whatever," she said.

Max kept working on his calculations.

"Max?" Luna said after a while. "Do you have to do all that math every time you time-travel?"

"Well," Max said, "you have to figure out your time coordinates for every destination. But I've added some new features to Timebender, like an auto-return key. After you arrive at your destination, just hit the ESCAPE key and ten seconds later, *poof!* Timebender pops back to the time and place it came from."

Luna's eyes lit up. "Oh," she said. "The ESCAPE key,

hmm?" She glanced at Max's notebook and saw that he had filled the page with scribbly looking calculations. "You really understand all that mumbo jumbo?"

"Sure," Max said. "Math is easy for me. It's spelling that messes me up." He punched the time coordinates into the keypad. The numbers appeared on the dashboard displays. "Okay," he said. "We're ready."

Max leaned out the open window and looked at Grady and Allie. "Back in five minutes," he said. "Promise."

Allie frowned. "Sounds like 'famous last words,'" she said.

Grinning, Max pressed ENTER on the keyboard, then counted, "Ten . . . nine . . . eight . . ."

One moment, the shiny orange VW Beetle was there. Seconds later, it wasn't. There was a *whoosh!*—the sound of air rushing to fill a vacuum.

Toby frowned. "I get the next trip," he said.

Grady checked his watch.

Allie shivered and hugged herself. "This is so wrong," she said.

Max and Luna looked out the windows of the Volkswagen Beetle. One moment, it was a bright October afternoon in the twenty-first century. The next moment, it was completely dark outside.

"It's really true!" Luna gasped.

"Didn't you believe me?" Max asked.

"Until you *do* it," Luna said, "time travel doesn't seem real." She looked around. "It's so dark!"

"I have a flashlight under the seat," Max said. "A real bright one."

Max reached under the passenger seat and pulled out a big, heavy-duty flashlight. He flicked it on, the light bouncing off Luna's wristwatch.

"Something's wrong with my watch," she said. "It shows the same time as when we left."

"Of course it does," Max said. "Your watch is still on twenty-first-century time. It doesn't know we've gone back to 1939."

Luna looked around. "Well, what time do you think it is?" she said.

"This time of year," Max said, looking all around, "the sun usually sets by five-thirty, and it's dark by six. I'd say it's at least seven o'clock right now—maybe later. I guess that's not 'fivish,' like you asked for, but it's the best I could do."

Max thrust the flashlight out the open window on the driver's side and shone it around like a spotlight. Its glare flickered across the broad lawn and the tangled sticklike branches of the surrounding walnut grove. It was hard to tell much about their surroundings with only a flashlight to see by. Still, Max could tell that everything was different.

Compared with the neatly trimmed backyard lawn they had just left, this lawn was wild and overgrown with weeds. Farther off, the big Victorian-style house was dark and deserted-looking. Its windows were boarded up and weeds grew up higher than the back porch.

"Luna, why did you pick 1939?" Max asked.

"Let's get out and look around," Luna said, ignoring Max's question.

Max opened the door and stepped out of the car. While his back was turned, Luna lifted the keyboard and ran her hands over the keys. It was too dark to see, but she knew that the ESCAPE key was located in the upper left-hand corner of the keyboard. She pressed the ESCAPE key, then got out of the car.

Max stood with his back to the Volkswagen, shining the flashlight around the yard. Then he heard a sound behind him: *Whoosh!*—the sound of air rushing to fill a vacuum.

He whirled around and pointed the flashlight at Luna. She had a strange look on her face—like a grin of triumph.

Then Max flashed the light beam over the bare spot next to Luna, where the car had been just seconds before. Timebender was gone.

2

STRANDED IN TIME

Grady plucked a clover out of the lawn, looked at it, then tossed it away. Allie gazed at the clouds. Toby stood and hummed some annoying tune.

The air shimmered and the orange VW Beetle appeared. Timebender had returned less than a minute after it left.

Allie stared in horror. The car was empty.

"What—!" Grady said. "Where are Max and Luna?"

"Dude!" Toby said.

"Oh, no!" Allie wailed while wringing her hands. "What happened to Max and Luna?"

Max flashed the light across the grass where Timebender had just stood. "I—I must have accidentally pressed the

ESCAPE key!" he said. "How could I be so stupid?"

Luna grinned then said smugly, "You didn't do anything wrong. *I* pressed the ESCAPE key."

Max stared at her. "You mean you accidentally—"

"No, Max," Luna said. "On purpose."

Max felt sick and angry at the same time. "Luna! Do you know what you did? You stranded us here! We've got no way home!"

Luna shrugged. "Come with me," she said calmly.

"Where?" Max asked.

Luna snatched the flashlight out of his hands and walked past him. "Just come with me."

Max gritted his teeth and followed Luna through the dark yard. "Luna! What's going on?!"

"You'll know soon enough," Luna said, shining the light on their path. They crossed the lawn toward the dark, deserted house, pushing their way through waist-high weeds. As they got closer to the house, they came to an overgrown hedge of juniper. Luna shone the light around until she found a narrow gap in the hedge. "This way," she said, taking the lead. Needle-shaped leaves scratched Luna and Max as they pushed their way through the gap.

"Your house sure is run-down," Luna said.

Max was already mad at Luna—and that comment didn't help his mood one bit. "It's not run-down," he said crossly. "It's just closed up. I remember my dad saying the house was closed up for a while in the late 1930s when my great-grandfather moved to Arizona."

Luna shone the light at the side of the house as they walked through the weeds. The circle of light played across cobwebs, peeling paint, broken shingles, and loose boards. "I like old houses like this one," she said. "Who fixed it up?"

Max paused and looked at the house. "My grandfather, Horton McCrane. When he came back from England after World War II, he repaired the place and filled it with antiques and stuff when he moved in." Max stopped walking and Luna looked back at him.

Luna shone the flashlight in Max's face. He shielded his eyes with his hands and squinted. "Hey!" he said. "Point that someplace else!"

"What's your problem, Max?" Luna said. "You're acting all grouchy!"

"Oh, excuse me for being grouchy!" Max said sarcastically. "You only stranded me here in 1939! That's nothing to get annoyed about, is it?"

"Look, Max," Luna said calmly. "I'm stranded here, too, and you don't see me panicking and getting all upset. So just calm down. Everything's going to be all right. You'll see." She turned around and continued walking.

Max was about to reply, but he bit off his words with clenched teeth. He followed Luna, stamping angrily.

When they reached the front of the house, Max felt a

surge of hope. The room his father used as a study was just on the other side of the wall—and that was where the time portal Max called "the Doorway to Doom" should be! *If I could get into the house*, he thought, *I could use the Doorway to get home!*

Then he remembered: His grandfather didn't bring the Doorway over from England until 1945. *Face it,* Max thought to himself, *you're stuck in 1939 and there's no way back—until that doorway arrives in six years!*

Max glanced at Luna up ahead of him, and his anger smoldered. *She's so smug!* he thought. *She acts like she's got a plan for getting back home—but what?*

When they got to the front of the house, Max peered around the yard, trying to make out familiar landmarks. It was hard to see anything by the dim starlight and the faint glimmer of moonlight in the east. Luna waved the flashlight around and Max saw that Mirabilis Way, which was a broad asphalt-paved street in Max's own time, was nothing but a narrow dirt road in 1939.

Looking toward the town, Max saw that his entire neighborhood was gone. Across the street, where a row of homes stood in his own time, Max could dimly make out a fruit orchard. All along the street were nothing but fields, trees, and a fenced-in cow pasture—not another house in sight.

"Everything's so different," he said in an awed voice.

"Duh!" Luna said. "There's a lot of time between our time and this time. Things change."

They walked into the middle of the dirt road. Off to the east, rising over some low hills beyond the cow pasture, was a yellow harvest moon, looking like a big glowing pumpkin.

"Now what?" Max said.

"We go that way." Luna pointed down the dirt road. "Toward town."

"Come on, Luna," Max said in exasperation. "Tell me what's going on!"

"You'll see," Luna said as she started walking toward town.

Max kicked a dirt clod, then followed after her.

Toby took off his backpack and sat in the driver's seat of the VW.

"Don't touch anything, Toby," Grady said, standing a few yards from the car.

"I'm not hurting anything!" Toby said.

"Grady," Allie said, "we have to take Timebender and rescue Max and Luna."

Grady looked at Allie in disbelief. "Do you know how to operate Timebender?" he asked. "Because I sure don't!"

"I don't know how to do the time calculations," Allie said, "but I know which buttons make it go."

Grady rolled his eyes. "Great! You know just enough to

get us as lost as they are! Face it, Allie. We can't operate Timebender without Max."

Allie thought for a moment, then said, "Hey! Let's tell Max's dad! Dr. McCrane is really smart. He could do the calculations."

"Max said his dad is at some conference in Chicago all weekend," Grady said.

"Oh, yeah," Allie said. "And there's no point telling Mrs. McCrane."

"Right," Grady said. "She'd faint dead away."

"Hey, Stubblefield, O'Dell!" Toby called from the car. "What's this for?" He held up a spiral-bound notebook.

"Toby," Grady said, "I told you not to touch anything!"

Allie's eyes lit up. "Hey!" she said. "Max's notebook!" She dashed to the car and snatched it out of Toby's hand.

"Dude!" Toby said. "Don't grab!"

Grady ran up behind Allie and looked over her shoulder.

"These are Max's calculations," she said.

"Looks like scribbling to me," Grady said.

"Yeah," Allie said. "But if we can figure out which of these numbers are the time coordinates Max punched into the Timebender displays, we can follow Max and Luna right to 1939."

"But look at that page!" Grady said. "There are numbers all over it! Which ones are the time coordinates?"

"We can ignore all of the formulas," Allie said. "The

time coordinates are a six-digit group of numbers like those. And those. And those."

"Oh, man," Grady said. "It could be any one of those sets of numbers. What if we pick the wrong ones?"

Allie thought for a moment—then she looked up, grinning broadly, her braces glittering in the sun. "Grady! It's so simple!"

Grady frowned. "It is?"

"Sure!" Allie said. "We just try one set of numbers, and if they're wrong, we hit the auto-return key, come back here, and try the next set."

Grady jumped up and pulled Allie to her feet. "Let's go!" They dashed to the car, where Toby sat behind the steering wheel with the driver's door open.

"Out, Toby!" Grady said. "Allie and I need Timebender. We're going to bring Max and Luna back."

"Cool," Toby said smugly. "I'm going, too."

"What?" Allie said. "Toby, you *hate* time travel!"

"Correction," Toby said. "I *used to* hate time travel. Now that I'm an official Timebender myself, I *love* time travel. Can't get enough of it."

"Get out of the car, Toby," Grady said. "We don't have time to mess around. You're staying here. That's final."

"I don't think so!" Toby snapped, slamming the door shut.

"Hey!" Grady said. "You almost caught my fingers in the door!"

Toby leaned his head out the window. "Dude! If it wasn't for me, you wouldn't even have McCrane's notebook! You owe me! If you dorks are going to 1939, then I am, too!"

"But why?" Allie asked.

Smirking, Toby pulled a thick paperback book from his backpack and handed it through the window to Allie. It was the *Comic Book Price Guide*. "Look at the line I circled on page 72."

Allie opened the book to page 72 and read, "'*Detective Comics* No. 27, published in 1939, first appearance of Batman—price: $35,000'!" Allie rolled her eyes. "Our friends are missing, and all you can think of is *money?*"

"A *lot* of money," Toby said. "Dude, those things sold for ten cents each—and if I can stuff my backpack full of brand-new 1939 comics, I'll be a millionaire!"

"Look, Toby," Allie said, "Max didn't invent Timebender to make you rich."

"Do I care?" Toby said. "Look, McCrane and his dorky time machine almost got me killed about half a dozen times. He owes me. And now that I'm an official Timebender, I intend to take a lot of trips, grab a lot of old comics, and make a ton of money." With that, Toby turned around and climbed into the backseat. "Well, what are you dorks waiting for?" he said. "Let's go!"

Grady scowled. "Whatever," he said. "Allie, you take the driver's seat."

"Right," Allie said. She slid in behind the steering wheel

and placed the keyboard across her lap. Grady walked around and got in on the passenger side.

"God," Allie prayed, "please help us find Max and Luna."

"Come on, come on," Toby said from the backseat. "Let's move this thing!"

Allie gasped.

Grady looked at her. "What?"

"I just remembered," she said. "That beat-up Volkswagen with all the flowers on it—they were sitting just like we are now: Allie and Grady in front, Toby in the back—and Max wasn't with them."

Toby leaned forward. "What are you losers talking about?"

"Allie," Grady said, "we've got no choice. We've got to get Max and Luna back, so let's just go, okay?"

"Yeah," Allie said. She punched the numbers into the keypad, then pressed ENTER. In ten seconds, Timebender would depart for another time.

"Allie," Grady said, "which is the auto-return key?"

"I think it's the BACKSPACE key," Allie said. She didn't look very sure.

Grady looked at Allie in astonishment. "You mean you *don't know?*"

Allie gasped. "I thought I did, but now I can't remember!" she said. "Grady, take out the batteries! Quick!"

But it was already too late.

Luna and Max walked down the dirt road for about half an hour before they reached the edge of town. By that time, the moon had risen above the rooftops. The few houses they passed were built in an old-fashioned style, but looked neat and freshly painted. There were Halloween decorations on many front porches—carved pumpkins, paper skeletons, and scarecrows stuffed with straw. A few trick-or-treaters were going house-to-house, wearing ghost costumes made from bedsheets, or witch costumes with pointed hats and brooms, or cowboy costumes with ten-gallon hats and toy six-shooters.

Max fumed as he walked alongside Luna. He also began to wheeze—his asthma always flared up when he got angry. He took his inhaler from his pocket and took a puff. He was not only furious with Luna for stranding them in 1939, he was also furious about her haughty silence. Finally, he could stand it no longer. As they passed under a streetlight, Max stopped.

"Luna," he said, "just tell me what your plan is! I *really* want to get back and see my family and friends again."

"Don't worry," she said. "We'll get back."

"How?" Max said.

"Trust me," Luna said.

"I got into this mess by trusting you," Max said bitterly.

Allie looked out the windshield of Timebender—and gasped.

"Grady!" she said. "Grady, look!"

Grady looked. They were sitting on the lawn behind the old Victorian house, but everything else was changed. The grove of walnut trees that surrounded the McCrane back-yard was gone. In place of the trees were buildings—but buildings like they had never seen before. They were tall, thirty or forty stories high. Some were made of translucent white stone, others of gold-tinted glass.

It seemed to be morning now instead of afternoon. The McCrane backyard had been transformed into a park, with a fountain in the middle.

"Dude!" Toby said, pointing. "Look up there!"

Allie and Grady looked. Up in the sky were hovercars—hundreds of them. Most were white or gold in color. They flew in precise, orderly lanes, as if traveling on invisible highways in the sky, and they gave off a faint but steady humming sound.

"Where are we?" Allie asked. "This sure isn't 1939."

"We didn't go back in time," Grady said. "This is the future."

Allie gasped again and pointed. "Look at Max's house!"

Grady looked, rubbed his eyes, then looked again. "I'm going to get a closer look," he said at last. He opened the door and stepped out. Allie and Toby followed.

The three time travelers stood beside the VW Beetle and

stared at Max's house without saying a word. The entire three-story Victorian house was completely enclosed within a huge egg-shaped bubble of clear crystal.

"Whoa!" Toby said in an awestruck voice.

"What's up with *that?*" Grady asked.

Allie shook her head slowly. "This," she said, "is too weird!"

"Hello there!" a man's voice called.

The time travelers turned. A man walked across the lawn toward them. His hair was shaped in a strange style that seemed almost like an abstract sculpture. It was swept out to a point in front, formed birdlike wings on the sides, and drifted behind in graceful, feathery wisps. Most striking of all, his hair was golden—not that shade of blond that is often *called* golden, but a true, shiny, metallic gold. His clothing was loosely draped, like a Roman toga, and made of overlapping layers of white-and-gold cloth.

"Is this vehicle a new exhibit?" the golden-haired man asked, pointing to Timebender.

"Exhibit?" Allie asked.

"Ah!" the golden-haired man said, eyeing the time travelers closely. "I see! You're all part of the exhibit! The three of you look just like them!"

"Like who?" Grady asked.

"Max McCrane's friends, of course," the man said. "You look exactly like Grady Stubblefield. And you, young lady—with that red hair and those braces, you look exactly like Allie O'Dell. And this one here—Toby Brubaker, of course. But where is Max McCrane?"

"That's what we'd like to know," Allie said.

The man laughed. "Oh, I get it!" he said. "This is a re-enactment! You're all actors pretending to be the real Allie, Grady, and Toby—and this machine is a perfect replica of Timebender! You all look exactly like the images in the history tapes. What a creative new exhibit for the museum!"

"Museum?" Allie asked. "What museum?"

"The McCrane Museum, of course," the man said, pointing to a sign next to the bubble-encased house. The sign read:

The McCrane Museum
◇

Childhood Home of Maxfield McCrane, Discoverer of the Timebender Principle

---

"Well, look at that," Allie said. "Here in the future, Max is some kind of historical figure—like Thomas Edison."

"Dude!" Toby said in disgust. "They treat McCrane like some kind of hero!"

"Give it a rest, Toby," Grady said. "You're just jealous because—Uh-oh! Looks like we're attracting a crowd."

It was true. People were approaching Timebender with

curious expressions on their faces. They were all dressed like the golden-haired man—white-and-gold robes, with golden-metallic hair sculpted in strange and graceful shapes. White and gold appeared to be the style of the future.

"Allie," Grady said softly but urgently, "I think we'd better get back to our own time and try again."

"No argument," Allie said. "Everybody back in the car and let's get—"

"Dude!" Toby said, pointing to the sky. "Look!"

Allie and Grady glanced up. A black-and-white hover-car was floating down out of the sky, coming straight toward them. The hovercar had a transparent dome on top, and two expressionless metal faces could be seen inside the dome. Allie and Grady recognized those faces.

The Time Troopers were coming.

"Oh, I love that movie!" Luna said.

Up ahead, Max saw the marquee of the Royal Theatre shining in the early evening darkness. It read:

JUDY GARLAND

in

THE WIZARD OF OZ

Max had always thought of it as "the old Royal," because it was shabby, abandoned, and boarded up in his day. In 1939, however, it looked shiny and new, freshly painted and brightly lit, with signboards on the pavement proclaiming, "MGM's Technicolor Triumph!" and "The Greatest Picture in the History of Entertainment."

Max and Luna walked up to the theatre. Luna paused to admire the colorful posters depicting Dorothy, the Tin Man, the Scarecrow, the Cowardly Lion, and the green-skinned Wicked Witch of the West. "Are you a good witch—or a bad witch?" Luna said to nobody in particular, doing a pretty good impression of Glinda, the "good witch" in the movie.

Luna turned to Max. "I know you don't believe me, Max," she said, "but there *are* good witches. I know, because I *am* a good witch."

"Tricking people to get what you want," Max said. "Is that what 'good witches' do?"

Luna rolled her eyes.

"Witchcraft may seem like a good thing at first," Max said. "You may think you're controlling forces and spirits. But before it's over, the forces and spirits end up controlling *you*."

"You *religious* people are so narrow-minded!" Luna sniffed. "You just can't tolerate people with different ideas, can you?"

"That's not fair, and you know it," Max said. "You and I have had lots of talks about astrology and witchcraft and all that weird stuff you're into. Have I ever been mean to you? Have I ever been rude or— What are you staring at?"

"This," Luna said. Without warning, she reached up and snatched the simple gold cross that hung around Max's neck.

"Hey!" Max said. "You broke the chain!"

Luna clutched the gold cross in her fist. "Oh, poor, poor Max!" she taunted. "You feel lost without your little good-luck charm, hmm?"

"I don't wear it for luck," Max said. "It's a symbol of the Name I believe in. That cross represents what He went through for me—and for you, too."

Luna laughed, dangling the cross in front of Max. "That Name, this cross, your God—none of that means anything to me," she said.

"If it means nothing to you," Max said, "give it back."

Luna stuck the cross in a pocket. "I don't want you wearing something that might offend . . . the person we're going to meet."

"Offend what person?" Max said.

"You'll see," Luna said.

They walked past the theatre and down to the corner, then turned left. Across the street, on their right, was the university campus. Up ahead was a row of two-story brownstone buildings. Roving bands of trick-or-treaters haunted the sidewalks—ghosts, vampires, princesses, monsters, and witches, all carrying sacks of goodies they had collected door-to-door.

Suddenly, Max stopped and slapped his forehead. "Oh, no!" he groaned.

Luna paused, looking impatient. "What's wrong?"

"I just had a horrible thought," Max said. "What if Allie

and Grady try to rescue us?" Max said. "If they come after us in Timebender, they'll get lost for sure!"

"We don't need to be rescued," Luna said with a shrug. "Come on. It's just up the block." She turned and continued along the sidewalk.

Max sighed. He had no choice but to trudge after her.

The Time Trooper hovercar settled toward the ground, coming straight toward Allie, Grady, and Toby.

"They've seen us!" Grady said, giving Allie and Toby a push. "Back to the car!" He turned and saw more golden-haired people had gathered around the car, both men and women.

"Excuse us!" Allie shouted.

"Coming through!" Grady shouted.

"Out of my way, losers!" Toby shouted, pushing people aside.

The golden-haired people parted. Grady ran around to the far side of the car while Toby and Allie jumped in the driver's side.

"Time travelers from the twenty-first century!" said an electronic voice. "Step out of the vehicle!" The Time Trooper hovercar floated above the ground a few yards away.

Allie pulled the door shut and placed the keyboard across her lap.

Grady slid into the passenger seat. "Power on!" Grady yelled, his voice cracking. He reached over and tapped random numbers into the keypad. The numbers appeared on the dash display. "Hit ENTER," he said, "and get us out of here!"

Allie hit ENTER, then looked out the window. Doors opened on both sides of the hovercar and ramps extended toward the ground. Two black-and-white Time Troopers dashed down the ramps, each holding a pistol-shaped device. Lettered across the chest of one robot was "TIME TROOPER 7" and across the chest of the other was "TIME TROOPER 11." Golden-haired people stepped out of the way of the Troopers.

In the backseat, Toby wailed in terror. In the driver's seat, Allie prayed. In the passenger seat, Grady counted down, ". . . three . . . two . . ."

The Time Troopers approached the driver's side of the orange Volkswagen. One of them reached for the door handle—

And grabbed empty air. The Volkswagen was gone.

Max and Luna climbed the steps of a huge old brownstone building. The entrance to the building was a recessed archway. Above the arch was a plaque fashioned of reddish-brown terra cotta, announcing in large, molded letters: HYDE BUILDING. A grinning stone gargoyle sat at the top of the arch, leering at Max and Luna as they passed beneath it.

They paused in front of a massive carved door with a big brass door-knocker. A brass plate on the door read: *Madame Jacquelynn Hyde,* Seer and Sorceress—Spells, Love Potions, Fortunes, Tarot Cards, and Palm Reading.

Luna grasped the brass knocker and gave it three hard whacks. They waited. Finally, there was a rattling sound at the latch. The door opened a few inches. A man's face appeared in the opening—an old man with white hair. "Yes?" the man said.

"We've come to see Madame Hyde," Luna said.

"Madame Hyde sees no one without an appointment," the man replied.

"But I'm a witch!" Luna said.

"A witch?" the man said. He looked Luna up and down, noting her purple designer top, purple dangles and bracelets, purple purse, and purple lip gloss. "Not much of a costume, is it?" he sneered. "Madame Hyde does not receive trick-or-treaters, either. Good night."

The door began to close—but Luna stuck her foot in the opening. "We are not trick-or-treaters, Mr. Woothering," Luna said. "I'm a *real* witch, and I'm here on business— witchcraft business."

Max noticed the man seemed startled that Luna called him by name. "I will tell Madame you are here," the man said, "but I do not think she will receive you."

Luna removed her foot and the man closed the door, leaving Max and Luna outside.

"How did you know that man's name?" Max asked.

"Madame Hyde mentions him in the book," Luna said.

"What book?" Max asked.

Luna didn't answer. Max decided he would find out soon enough.

Minutes passed. Finally, the door swung wide open.

Mr. Woothering stood in the doorway, dressed in a black tuxedo and white starched shirt and collar. He was old and thin, with sunken cheeks and dark, shadowy eyes. His eyebrows were white and bushy. His hair was white, wispy, and stood straight up. He stared at Luna, then at Max.

"Madame will see you," he said in a tone of disapproval.

Luna and Max entered, and Mr. Woothering closed the door behind them with a *thud!* that echoed throughout the building.

Max looked all around and saw a vast rectangular atrium, an enclosed type of courtyard. At either end were broad staircases with marble stairs and intricate ornamental ironwork. The building rose on all sides around the atrium, three stories high, with elaborate ironwork balustrades lining the landing of each floor. Overhead was a skylight made of hundreds of panes of glass set into an iron grillwork.

"I am Madame Hyde," said a woman's voice above them. Max and Luna looked up as a woman in her mid-thirties descended the staircase, one hand lightly touching the iron railing. Dressed in a simple white gown tied at the waist with a black cord, she had raven-black hair and skin as pale and smooth as sculpted marble. Her eyes were large, deep, and blue. Her form was slender, and her face thin, with high cheekbones and lips the color of blood.

Luna's eyes were wide with excitement, as if she were in the presence of royalty. "My name is Luna Skyes," she said. "And this is Max McCrane."

The woman walked up to Max and Luna, examining them keenly. She turned to the white-haired man. "That will be all, Woothering," she said.

"Yes, Madame." He turned and walked away, his footsteps echoing.

Madame Hyde stared at Luna. "Should I know you?"

"No," Luna said. "But I know you. I've read your book a dozen times."

"My dear girl," the woman said, "I have never written a book."

"You're writing a book right now," Luna said. "In fact, it's almost finished and ready to send to a publisher. Your book will be snapped up by the first publisher you send it to, and it will come out in the bookstores next year—1940."

"Luna," Max said in horror. "Don't tell her about the future!"

But Luna kept talking. "Your book," she said, "will be

printed and reprinted for many years. And it will look like this—"

Luna opened her purse and pulled out a paperback book. The cover had a black-and-white photo of a woman on it— Madame Hyde herself. Printed across the top of the book were these words: *The Wisdom of Witchdom* by Madame Jacquelynn Hyde.

Madame Hyde reached for the book with trembling hands. She ran her hands over the cover, then slowly opened the book and read the first few sentences. Her face paled. She snapped the book shut and looked at Luna with wide, frightened eyes.

"This *is* my book!" she said in a stunned whisper. "I wrote these words! But how is this possible? My book is an unfinished manuscript!" She gulped hard. "Where did this come from?"

"The same place *we* came from," Luna said. "The future."

◎ ◎ ◎

The forest was cool and quiet, shaded by tall sequoia red-wood trees, some of which were several thousand years old. In a clearing in the middle of the forest, furry brown shrews with pointed snouts crept among the tall grasses, snuffling for insects and slugs to eat.

The quiet in the clearing was broken by the sound of a herd of woolly mammoths crashing through the forest. There were fifteen of the beasts, and they were huge, elephant-like, and covered with shaggy brown hair. Most had six- to eight-foot-long tusks, but the largest bull of the herd weighed over nine tons and wielded twelve-foot-long tusks. It reared its trunk in the air and roared, then led its herd out into the clearing.

The air in the middle of the clearing shimmered, but the mammoths didn't notice. Something orange took shape and solidified, gleaming in the sun. Timebender had arrived.

Allie and Grady stared out the windshield as the herd of shaggy mammoths plodded by, just a few yards away. Toby pressed his pasty face against the window. "Dude!" he said in a trembling voice. "Where are we?"

"I don't know," Grady said, "but we're a long way from where we want to be. Those aren't elephants, are they? They look like—"

"Mammoths," Allie said. "We studied about them in Miss Hinkle's science class. They lived in the Pleistocene Epoch, and they've been extinct for about ten thousand years."

"Great!" Grady said. "We're lost in time again!"

◎ ◎ ◎

Time Trooper 7 sat in the left-hand seat, operating the controls and guiding the hovercar through the surging timestream. Trooper 11 sat in the right-hand seat, its attention focused on the glowing screen of the chronoscope. Shifting clouds of brilliant color swirled beyond the transparent bubble canopy.

"I am tracking the chronon emissions from the time-bending vehicle," Trooper 11 said. "The fugitives are diving deep into the timestream—about twelve-point-three kilo-years in the past. It will take five to ten minutes to pinpoint their exact position in time."

"And then we'll have them," Trooper 7 said. "This time, they won't get away."

4

THE BIG HAIRY FENDER-BENDER

Madame Hyde gave Max and Luna a brief tour around the first floor of the atrium. One room was a large library filled with books on witchcraft, astrology, and the occult arts. Another room was a museum-like place containing everything from suits of armor to ancient weapons to paintings and statues. Max couldn't help thinking that, to afford all of these things, Madame Hyde must make an awful lot of money telling fortunes and casting spells.

Finally, Madame Hyde brought Max and Luna to a darkened room she called "the crystal parlor." As Max and Luna crossed the threshold, Madame Hyde stood beside the door, still holding the book that Luna had brought from the future. She waved her arms and called out, "Alight!"

Instantly, flames lit up two dozen candles all around the room. A crackling fire sprang up in a large fireplace of carved marble. The firelight cast a soft, eerie glow around the room, filling Luna's eyes with sparklets of light.

Max looked at Madame Hyde. "A magic trick, huh?" he said. "Very cool."

"Cool?" the woman said, looking baffled.

"In our time," Luna said, "'cool' means 'impressive.'"

"Ah," Madame Hyde said.

Max looked around the room. The walls were hung with antique tapestries, and the room was furnished with plush chairs and a red velvet sofa. There were also instruments of the occult arts, including an astrolabe for locating celestial bodies, a thirteenth-century brass torquetum for measuring astronomical coordinates, and a celestial globe.

"Madame Hyde," Luna said, "Max is a cowan."

Max frowned. "What's a 'cowan'?"

"An outsider, a normal," Madame Hyde said. "A non-witch."

"He's also an unbeliever," Luna said.

"Ah!" Madame Hyde said, rubbing her hands together. "Unbelievers are a challenge—and I *love* a challenge."

"I'm not an 'unbeliever,'" Max said. "It's just that I only believe in things I *know* are true."

"Young man," Madame Hyde said, "there are truths in this universe which you can scarcely imagine!"

"Max," Luna said, "do you know the difference between M-A-G-I-C and M-A-G-I-C-K?"

Max shrugged.

"Magic with a C is stage magic," Luna said. "You know—illusions, sleight of hand, pulling a rabbit out of a hat. But magick with a K is the real deal."

"Your friend is correct, young man," Madame Hyde said. "The magick I practice is not an illusion. I summon spirits and forces to do my bidding."

"I don't know how you lit those candles," Max said. "But whether you used magic with a C or magick with a K, you used deception. Magic with a C is fun because it fools the eyes. But magick with a K is dangerous, because it fools the soul."

Madame Hyde smiled craftily. "Well," she said. "I can see we are in for an interesting evening."

She pointed to a round table with several chairs. "Please," she said, "be seated."

A crystal ball rested on a brass pedestal in the center of the table. Since Max could see nothing else in the room that was made of crystal, he concluded that the crystal ball was the reason Madame Hyde called this room "the crystal parlor." Here, apparently, Madame Hyde received her clients and read their fortunes (and probably emptied their bank accounts of a fortune as well).

Max and Luna took chairs across the table from each other.

"So, Luna, Max," Madame Hyde said, "tell me about yourselves. Why have you come—and how did you get here from the future?"

"You *do* believe me, don't you?" Luna asked. "You do believe that we really did come from the twenty-first century?"

"I'm not completely sure," Madame Hyde said. Then she held up the paperback copy of *The Wisdom of Witchdom*. "But this," she said, "is very convincing evidence in your favor. Tell me how you came here."

"Max invented a time machine," Luna said. "He calls it Timebender—"

Max interrupted. "Luna *tricked* me into bringing her to 1939 in Timebender. Apparently, she wanted to meet you."

"That's right," Luna said. "Madame Hyde, after I read your book, I just *had* to meet you. I want to become a witch like you. I want to become your disciple, your apprentice, so you can teach me all about the craft."

"I'm flattered," Madame Hyde said, smiling. "And I'm also curious. Tell me about this future you come from. What is the world like in the twenty-first century?"

Before Luna could answer, Max said, "You're the fortune-teller. Why don't *you* tell *us* about the future?"

Madame Hyde's eyes darkened. Her jaw muscles twitched.

"Max!" Luna said reproachfully. "You're being rude!"

"I'm serious!" Max said. "If she can foretell the future, let her show it to us in that crystal ball."

"When I read the future, dear boy," Madame Hyde said coldly, "I sense images, impressions, forms, shadows. It's not like watching a movie."

"He's hopeless, Madame Hyde," Luna said, glaring at Max. "Just ignore him." She turned to the woman. "The future I come from is a very cool place. You'd love it. Let's see. . . . We have computers, which look kind of like TVs, only—"

"TVs?" the woman said.

"Oh, that's right," Luna said. "You don't have TVs in 1939. Well, a TV is kind of like a radio with pictures. And a computer is like a typewriter with a TV attached."

"I see," Madame Hyde said, though she still appeared confused. "And these computers—what do you do with them?"

"Well," Luna said, "you can play games and do homework on them, and you can go on the Internet and send e-mail—"

"What kind of net?" Madame Hyde asked. "What kind of mail?"

Luna looked flustered. "It's kind of complicated to explain how the Internet works. But there are all kinds of other cool things in the future—movies on DVDs, space shuttles that take people into space, personal CD players, airplanes that fly faster than sound—" Luna stopped and looked at Madame Hyde.

The woman looked back in total bewilderment. "I'm sorry, dear," she said, "but I haven't the slightest idea what you're talking about."

Max chuckled. Luna turned a cold stare in his direction.

"I'm sorry," Max said, "but it's funny!"

"*What* is funny, young man?" Madame Hyde asked coldly.

"A fortuneteller," Max said, "who doesn't have a clue about the future!"

Madame Hyde's eyes narrowed. "Go ahead, young man," she said. "Laugh. Enjoy yourself. Make fun of that which you do not understand."

Max's laughter died and his smile faded. Suddenly, he sensed in this woman a very real threat.

"You will find," Madame Hyde continued, "that I am much more than a fortuneteller. I am a *witch*. And those who are wise know better than to laugh at a witch."

In the corner, a clock chimed eight o'clock.

Allie, Grady, and Toby got out of the Volkswagen and watched the shaggy mammoths lumber through the tall grass. "Are they dangerous?" Toby asked, his pasty skin even paler than usual.

"Maybe if they sit on you," Grady said. "But they don't eat people. Look at them. They're just munching on leaves and grass. They don't even notice us."

Allie giggled.

"What's funny?" Grady asked.

She giggled again. "What's shaggy and weighs eight or nine tons and goes around in circles?"

"What?" Grady asked.

"A mammoth stuck in a revolving door," Allie said.

"Dude!" Toby said. "That's stupid!"

"Allie," Grady said. "We're in trouble! This is no time for lame jokes!"

"I just want to keep our spirits up," Allie said. "Here's another: What's shaggy and has six legs, three ears, four tusks, and two trunks?"

Grady rolled his eyes. "I give up."

"A mammoth with spare parts," Allie said, cracking up.

Toby shook his head. "That's not even funny," he said.

"Just one more," Allie said. "How do you stop a mammoth from charging?"

"That's easy," Grady said. "Take away its credit cards."

Allie stared at something behind Grady. "No, I mean it! How do you stop a mammoth from charging? Look!"

Grady turned around. "No!" he shouted.

The big bull mammoth charged at the orange Volkswagen. Head low, tusks pointed forward, the mammoth slammed into the passenger side of the Volkswagen with a sound of crunching metal. The car rolled onto its side, then onto its top, then onto its other side. It came to rest, battered and dented, with its windows broken and the windshield cracked.

The mammoth snuffled around the overturned car with its trunk. Then it turned and galumphed away.

Max blinked. "You're—a *real* witch? You ride a broomstick and practice black magick?"

Madame Hyde smiled. "I own a broomstick, but I don't use it for transportation," she said. "And as for so-called 'black magick'—I'll have you know that all the magick I do is *white* magick, *good* magick, *harmless* magick. A good witch—"

"There's no such thing as a 'good witch,'" Max said, "and no such thing as 'good witchcraft.'"

"How sad," said Madame Hyde, "to see such narrow-mindedness in one so young."

Max shrugged. "Luna and I have spent a lot of time talking about this stuff. I've read up on witchcraft, and I know how dangerous it is. And I know that witchcraft is *wrong*. The Bible says that people who practice sorcery, tell fortunes, and practice witchcraft are doing things God hates—and they're destroying their own souls."

"I see," the woman said, leveling an intense stare at Max. "You believe in the Bible—that old book of fables and oppressive rules. You believe in a cruel and bloodthirsty God who allowed His own Son to be tortured and killed on a wooden cross."

"The God I know is the true God," Max began. He reached up, groping for the cross that always hung around his neck, but it was gone. He turned to Luna and said, "You have something that belongs to me."

Luna took the gold cross out of her pocket and slapped

it on the table. Max took it and held it up. "I know a God," he said, "who loves me so much that He gave His Son to die for me. And I know there is a cruel and bloodthirsty enemy in this world, Madame Hyde. You wear *his* symbol around *your* neck."

Madame Hyde reached up and fingered the golden ornament that hung at her throat—a pentacle, a five-pointed star enclosed in a circle. "This," she said proudly, "is the symbol of witchcraft—of *La Vecchia Religione*, the Old Religion. My religion is older than Christianity—older, more powerful, and more *real* than your musty collection of myths and creeds."

Max rolled his eyes. "Here we go again," he said.

"What do you mean?" Madame Hyde asked.

"I've heard all this before," Max said, "and it's totally bogus. Sure, there were witches and sorcerers before Jesus was born. But faith in the one true God goes all the way back to the Garden of Eden, when God created the first human beings. So don't try to tell me that your 'Old Religion' is older than faith in God, because it isn't. God's plan is older than time, older than space, older than the universe itself."

"You're only repeating words you heard in Sunday school," Madame Hyde said. "You don't even know that the Garden of Eden existed!"

Max threw his head back and laughed. "I know the Garden existed," he said, "because I've been there. I'm a time traveler, remember?"

Madame Hyde's eyes widened, as if she just had the most wonderful idea. "In that case," she said, "perhaps you would take me to the Garden in your time machine. If you would take me there, perhaps I would be persuaded to believe in your God and worship Him as you do."

Max glanced at Luna, and Luna glared back at him. "I can't take you there," Max said, turning back to Madame Hyde. "Luna sent our time machine back to the twenty-first century without us. And besides, I wouldn't do it if I could."

"I see," Madame Hyde said, frowning. She ran her hand over the shiny cover of *The Wisdom of Witchdom*. "On the one hand," she said, "we have this strange book—my own manuscript, completed and published, handed down to me from the future. On the other hand, you claim to have invented a time machine, but the machine itself is conveniently missing. Are you telling me the truth, or is this all some elaborate hoax? I wonder . . ."

"It's not a hoax," Luna said. "We really did come here in Max's time machine, and I did send it back to the twenty-first century."

"Believe it or not, it's the truth," Max said. "Just as sure as my faith in the one true God is the truth—and your 'Old Religion' is a lie."

Madame Hyde smiled slyly. "Before this night is over," she said, "we shall see which religion is true and which is a lie."

Grady, Allie, and Toby approached the overturned VW. Timebender had really taken a beating.

"Oh, Max's poor car!" Allie moaned. "All that work—a whole summer of pounding out dents, replacing glass, and repainting! Now, look at it! Totally trashed!"

"Oh, man," Grady said, "Max'll totally lose it when he sees this!"

"Dude!" Toby snorted. "Right now, a fender-bender with a big hairy elephant is the least of our problems!"

"Right," Allie said. "The thing we have to worry about is finding Max and Luna."

"Look," Toby said, "the thing *you* have to worry about is getting *me* back home!"

Grady glared at Toby.

"Everybody just chill, okay?" Allie said.

"He just better watch it," Grady muttered. He turned toward the battered Volkswagen and took a deep breath. "Well, for starters," he said, "we need to get Timebender back on its wheels." He walked around to the roofside of the overturned car. Allie followed him.

Toby backed away. "I'm not helping," Toby said. "You two got me into this mess, and you'd better get me out."

Grady scowled at Toby. "Look, Toby—Allie and I didn't even want you to come. You forced us to bring you along. So, get over here and lend a hand. *Now*."

Toby swore, then plodded over to the car.

"Okay," Grady said, "on the count of three. . . . One . . . two . . . *three!*"

They all pushed—though Toby didn't try very hard. The orange Volkswagen tilted slowly at first, then toppled onto its wheels, bouncing and squeaking on its old springs and bald tires.

Toby sat down in the tall grass. "I'm getting really sick of time-traveling with you losers," he said. "You get me into one jam after—*Yow!* Get them *off* me!" He jumped up and ran wildly through the grass, waving his arms. A swirling black cloud of insects swarmed around his head.

"Toby!" Grady shouted. "Toby, come back here!"

"Aaaaggghhh!" Toby wailed. "They're biting me!"

Grady took off after Toby.

Standing helplessly beside the VW, Allie watched Toby run helter-skelter, pursued by a swarm of insects.

"Toby!" Grady shouted. "Stop! You're running right into—"

"Ooof!" Toby hit something, then bounced off and landed on his back in the grass. He looked up and saw that he had collided with the big hairy haunches of the bull mammoth. The startled mammoth grunted in surprise, and turned its head toward Toby.

Twenty yards away, Grady skidded to a stop.

Lying on the ground, Toby was vaguely aware that the black swarm of insects was settling over him—huge mosquitoes, some with bodies fully an inch long. They landed on his arms and face, yet Toby scarcely noticed. He had bigger problems—mammoth-sized problems.

The bull mammoth eyed Toby with keen interest. Its massive white tusks swayed over him. Its trunk snuffled toward him. That trunk was studded with long, bristly hairs, and the nostrils at the end of the trunk glistened with mammoth mucus. Worse still, other mammoths were taking an interest in Toby. Their intelligent eyes sized Toby up, trying to figure out if the pasty-skinned human with the piggish green eyes and pudgy body was a threat to the herd.

Grady edged carefully toward Toby. "Toby," he said softly. "Don't panic!"

So, naturally, Toby panicked. A strangled cry of fright began deep in his throat, and finally exploded from his mouth—a shriek of mindless terror!

Startled, the bull mammoth retreated a step, reared up its trunk, and bellowed!

Toby screamed again!

The mammoth trumpeted again!

Toby scrambled to his feet, ran, stumbled, got up again—and then the bristly, slimy mammoth trunk slapped him down into the grass once more.

A few yards away, Grady decided to distract the beast. "Hey, you!" he yelled. "Leave him alone! Come get me! Hey!"

But the mammoths ignored Grady and closed in around Toby.

Allie ran out beside Grady and shouted along with him.

"Hey, Nosey! Yoo-hoo! Over here! Why don't you pick on somebody your own size!"

Grady stubbed his toe on something. He looked down and saw a football-shaped rock, about six inches long. He picked it up and threw it like a forward pass. The rock sailed in a perfect spiral, hitting the bull mammoth on the shaggy hump atop its head.

The beast didn't even notice.

Toby rolled over and crawled through the grass, his skin teeming with mosquitoes. The bull mammoth probed at him with its snaky snout. Shiny globs of mammoth slobber stained Toby's tee shirt and cargo pants. "Dude!" Toby wailed. "Don't squash me!"

"Oh, no!" Allie cried. "Grady, what do we do?"

Grady pointed. "Look! What's that?"

Four golden-brown blurs moved from the shade of some ancient sequoias. The blurs passed through the grass like ripples on water—some kind of animal, large and muscular, but mostly hidden by the grass. The animals moved steadily toward the mammoth herd. They emerged from the tall grass and Grady and Allie saw what they were:

Saber-toothed tigers.

"Now, Luna, dear," Madame Hyde said. "A few moments ago, you said you came here to learn more about the craft."

"Yes," Luna said eagerly. "I want to know everything I can about witchcraft. I want to be your disciple—your apprentice."

Madame Hyde smiled. "I've often thought it would be wonderful to have an apprentice," she said, "someone who would be like a daughter to me, someone to whom I could pass along my skills, my craft, my knowledge. But what about your parents? What about your friends? If you stay here with me, won't you be missed in your own time?"

"After I've learned all I can learn," Luna said, "I can return to my own time—and no one even has to know I was gone."

"How long do you wish to stay in my time?" the woman asked.

"Years, maybe," Luna said. "As long as it takes for me to become a great witch."

"Time for a reality check, Luna," Max said. "You don't have any way back to your own time."

"Don't be so dense, Max," Luna said. "I've already figured out how to get back to my own time."

"Oh, right," Max said with thick sarcasm. "Well, I wish you'd let me in on your secret for getting back to the twenty-first century."

"Madame Hyde," Luna said, "why don't you explain it to him?"

The woman appeared baffled. "Explain what, dear?"

"You know—the spell for traveling in time," Luna said. "It's in your book."

Max blinked in surprise. So did Madame Hyde.

"I tried the spell myself," Luna said, "but I must be doing something wrong, because it doesn't work for me."

"Hold it!" Max said. "Let me get this straight. Your plan for getting us back to our own time is . . . a magick spell?"

The saber-toothed tigers were heavily built, larger than African lions, but with shorter legs, closer to the ground. They didn't look like tigers—they were heavier and more muscular than tigers and had no stripes. Instead of long, swishing tiger tails, they had short bobtails. Their most impressive feature was a pair of curved swordlike upper fangs. Though these animals were not built for speed, their tusks were superbly designed for ripping and killing prey. The four big cats moved toward the mammoth herd.

Allie started forward. "We've got to get Toby!" she said.

Grady grabbed her arm and pulled her down into the grass. "Wait!" he said. "Those cats aren't interested in Toby. I don't think they even see him."

Grady was right. As if on a signal, all four cats went after one of the smaller mammoths at the edge of the herd. They pounced at the mammoth's side and hindquarters, keeping clear of its tusks. The mammoth turned, bellowing.

Allie cried out and hid her eyes.

Standing over Toby, the huge bull mammoth turned at the sound of its stricken herd-mate. At that moment, the bull and the other mammoths had a much bigger worry than a pudgy human from the future. Trumpeting a war cry, the bull mammoth led the charge against the big cats.

Grady seized the opportunity. Leaving Allie crouched in the grass, he dashed to Toby's side and grabbed him by the shirt. "Come on, Toby!" he said. "Let's get out of here!"

But Toby, hysterical with panic, flailed his arms, forcing Grady backward. Grady tripped and fell in the grass. Toby jumped up and took off across the clearing. He ran mindlessly past Allie and kept on going.

Grady picked himself up off the ground, turned, and saw Toby running straight toward Timebender. "Allie!" Grady called. "What's Toby doing?"

Allie looked back toward Timebender—and in an instant, she realized what Toby was about to do. "Toby, no!" she shouted.

Toby jumped in behind the wheel and grabbed the computer keyboard.

Allie sprinted toward Timebender. In seconds she reached the driver's-side door—but Toby had locked it. "Toby, let me in!" she called—but Toby ignored her.

Allie ran around and tugged at the badly crunched passenger-side door. It stuck for a moment, then groaned open. Allie jumped into the car and saw that the dashboard

displays were alight with glowing numbers. Toby had
already entered random coordinates! "Toby," she yelled,
"don't press ENTER!"

Toby looked at her with terror in his wide green eyes.
His short, stubbly hair stood out like wire bristles. "I
already did!" he squealed.

Grady sprinted toward Timebender. He saw Toby and
Allie in the front seat. Something was wrong. Even from a
distance, Grady could read the look of horror on Allie's face.

Almost there, just a few more yards—

Grady footsteps slowed, then stopped. He stared helplessly.

Somewhere behind him, there was a sound of struggle,
of clashing mammoth tusks and saber fangs, of mammoth
bellows and cat growls. But Grady didn't even notice.

"They left without me!" he said in a stunned voice.

Timebender was gone. Grady was alone in the Pleistocene forest.

5

CAPTURED!

"Toby Brubaker, you little creep!" Allie screamed, sitting in the passenger seat of the Volkswagen Beetle. "Grady went out there to save *your* life—and you *left* him there!"

Toby sat behind the steering wheel. "Dude!" he said. "It's not my fault!"

Allie slapped his face.

"Ow!" Toby yelled, cringing against the door. "What did you hit me for?"

"Mosquito," Allie said. "I killed it—see?" She plucked the dead mosquito off Toby's face.

"Oh," Toby said, relaxing. "Thanks."

"Don't thank me!" Allie's eyes flashed with fury. "I'm so mad at you, I could—"

"But it's not my fault!"

"Oh, right, Toby!" Allie said. "Nothing's *ever* your fault!"

"Dude!" Toby said, putting his face in his hands. "Everybody's always against me! Why do I always get blamed whenever—"

Allie slapped him again.

"Ow!" Toby recoiled from Allie.

Allie picked off another dead mosquito and showed it to him. "Admit it, Toby," she said. "For once in your life, admit that you're a selfish, cowardly little weasel!"

Toby scowled sullenly.

"You know what?" Allie said. "If I had been five seconds slower getting back to the car, you would have left me behind, too! You don't care about anyone but—"

"Dude! Look!" Toby pointed out the driver's-side window. Allie looked through the broken glass—

And saw the McCrane House.

Allie looked around the yard. Walnut groves bordered the broad lawn. From the location of the sun, it appeared to be early morning.

"Hey!" Toby said. "I did it! I got us back to our own time!"

"No," Allie said. "Look at those trees—they're a lot younger than when we left. This isn't our own time. It's not even close."

Madame Hyde stood up from the table. She seemed shaken. "Luna," she said, "are you telling me that you sent

Max's time machine away because you believed a magick spell would take you home?"

"Of course," Luna said. "The time-travel spell is right there in your book—page 147."

Madame Hyde opened the book with trembling fingers, flipping to page 147. "Yes," she said, sinking back in her chair, "I remember writing that spell."

Luna looked perplexed. "You remember . . . *writing* it? But in the book you said you learned that spell from a great sorcerer, Xander Mordin. You used that spell to visit ancient Egypt and Rome and—"

"Yes, yes," Madame Hyde said hastily. "I mean, I remember writing that spell exactly as it was given to me by Xander himself."

"Yeah, right," Max muttered.

"But why doesn't the spell work for me?" Luna asked.

"Well," said the woman, "did you make all the preparations? Did you ring a silver bell three times?"

"Yes," Luna said. "And I held the herbs in my hands, just as it says in the book—a sprig of rosemary in my right hand, a sprig of parsley in my left. Then I said the spell: 'By count of one, my spell's begun / By count of two, Time's power undo / By count of three, I grasp the key / By count of four, I'm through the door / By count of five, I have arrived / By count of six, the clock unticks / By count of seven, the gift is given / By count of eight, the past awaits / By count of nine, the future's mine / By count of ten, I'm anywhen! / Obey my will and heed my rhyme / Open to me, doors of Time!'"

"Give me a break," Max muttered.

Madame Hyde arched one eyebrow toward Max. "Were there any unbelieving *cowans* present when you said the spell?" she asked.

"No," Luna said. "I was alone in my room."

"I see," Madame Hyde said. "Well, sometimes a spell needs a little added boost in order to work."

"Oh?" Luna said. "Like what?"

"The next time you try the time-travel spell, try raising both hands to the sky and chanting, 'By tick, by tock, turn back the clock!'"

"Yeah," Max said, "or maybe you should bury a wristwatch in the ground under a full moon, sneeze three times, then do the hokey-pokey. That'll work just as well."

Luna scowled. "Max McCrane, you're being rude and stupid!"

"Luna, all this abracadabra stuff is ridiculous," Max said. "Look, time travel is a matter of physics. You can't time-travel by waving your arms in the air and chanting some silly rhyme. Luna, Madame Hyde is a fraud. She never time-traveled to ancient Egypt or anywhere else. She wrote that book for superstitious people like you—and she did it to make a quick buck. Don't you know when someone's making a fool of you?"

Luna's eyes flashed with anger and she started to speak— but Madame Hyde silenced her with an upraised hand.

"Luna, dear," the woman said, "I have had to deal with doubters and skeptics throughout my career. Perhaps the time has come to give your friend a *real* demonstration of my magickal powers."

Max didn't like the sound of that. "What kind of demonstration?" he asked.

Madame Hyde's eyes flashed. "Come with me," she said, "both of you."

Sweat beaded up on Grady's forehead. He was in big trouble—abandoned in time, stranded in a world of mammoths and saber-toothed cats. Allie and Toby were gone, and so was Timebender. There was no way Allie would ever find her way back to him.

Grady knew this was all Toby's doing—Allie would never have abandoned a friend. But Grady had no time to waste being mad at Toby. He had more urgent matters to think about. First order of business: survive. *I've got to hide!* he told himself. *If those saber-toothed cats see me, I'm dead meat!*

He hunched down, using the tall grass for cover as he sprinted toward the towering trees. He tried to imagine spending the rest of his life alone in a hostile world of prehistoric dangers. Then it occurred to him that the rest of his life might not be a very long time at all.

God, he prayed. *What am I doing here? Please, show me a way out of this mess!*

Then he heard a humming sound. It came from the sky, above and behind him. *Mosquitoes again!* he thought. The idea of being swarmed and bitten by a whole cloud of those bloodsucking bugs made his skin crawl.

Grady ran around behind one of the massive redwoods. His breath came in ragged gasps. He peered out from behind the tree—

And saw the Time Troopers!

The black-and-white hovercar settled down in the meadow—that was the humming sound he had heard, not mosquitoes. The vehicle hovered two feet off the ground, and the doors opened. The two Time Troopers hurried down the boarding ramps, each gripping a crystal-lensed pistol device.

At the far end of the clearing, the mammoths had fended off the attack by the sabertooths. The great bull mammoth continued to swing at the cats with its mighty tusks as the rest of the herd moved off among the trees.

One of the cats noticed the Time Troopers—and began prowling toward them. Soon, the other three saber-toothed cats followed. The bull mammoth, seeing that the battle was over, trumpeted its victory and rejoined the herd.

From behind the tree, Grady watched as the cats stalked the robots. Grady thought, *If those cats take a bite from the Time Troopers, they're in for a disappointment.*

The cat in the lead crept up toward the nearest Time

Trooper—Trooper 7. There was a long, tense moment of suspense as Trooper 7 raised its pistol device and pointed it at the cat.

The cat leaped! Grady expected Trooper 7 to fire at the cat, vaporizing it in midair. The pistol device didn't fire. The cat didn't vaporize. Instead, the cat fastened itself onto Trooper 7's metal arm.

Trooper 7 swung its arm over its head—cat and all. The saber-toothed tiger went flying. With an astonished scream, the huge cat landed in the grass about five yards away. The cat tumbled and rolled and finally came to a stop. The cat's eyes crossed. It looked stunned. It tried to stand—but fell over on its side.

The other three saber-toothed cats pounced, two on Trooper 7, one on Trooper 11. Within seconds, all went flying, landing within a few feet of their brother. Just as quickly as that, the fight was over. The four saber-toothed cats staggered away in defeat.

The two Time Troopers turned and looked at Grady. "You!" said Trooper 7. "Time traveler! Come out from behind that tree!"

Grady swallowed hard. Then he stepped out from behind the tree and faced the robots. With their crystal-lensed pistol devices pointed at him, the two Time Troopers walked toward him.

Allie and Toby came around to the front of the McCrane House—and stopped in their tracks. The house and neighborhood looked much as Allie remembered—but also very different. The iron fence in front of the house was there, and so was the asphalt-paved street Max lived on, Mirabilis Way. But where were the split-level homes with sloping front lawns that lined the street in Allie's own time? In their place were a bunch of houses under construction—wooden frames without walls or roofs.

There was a car parked at the curb in front of the McCrane House—a long, shiny, black car. The hood was almost six feet long, with a gleaming chrome hood ornament. The car had bulging, swept-back fenders front and back, with white-sidewall tires. It was an expensive-looking classic car, and neither Allie nor Toby had ever seen one like it before.

"Dude!" Toby said. "I'm starting to itch like crazy!" Big red mosquito-bite welts were rising on Toby's arms and face.

"Well, stop scratching," Allie said. "That just makes it worse."

"Hi!" a voice said behind them. Allie and Toby turned around—

And there was Max!

He was walking toward them from the house: a boy of about thirteen, with the same brown hair and brown eyes, the same round-lensed glasses, and walking with his hands in his pockets the same way Max always did. "Max!" Allie said. "Max, I can't believe it's really you!" She ran to him and threw her arms around him.

"Huh?" said the brown-haired boy, a startled look on his face. He wriggled out of Allie's hug. "My name's not Max—it's Ozzie! Who are you guys?"

Allie put her hand to her mouth. Looking closely, she could see that it wasn't Max, despite a close resemblance. Her heart sank. "Oh!" she said. "Oh, I'm sorry. I'm Allie and this is Toby. You look like someone we know."

"Ozzie?" Toby said, staring at the boy. "Dude! Your real name's Oswald, right? You're Max McCrane's dad!"

"Huh?" Ozzie said, looking baffled. "Sure, my name's Oswald—but only my parents call me that. And I'm not anybody's dad!"

"Don't mind Toby," Allie said. "He's always saying weird stuff like that." She paused. "You're going to think this is a dumb question, but—what year is it?"

"Huh?" said Ozzie. "Oh! It's a 1939."

Allie gasped. "Did you hear that, Toby?" she said excitedly. "It's 1939! That's the year Max and Luna were going to!"

Ozzie looked baffled. "What are you talking about?"

"Ozzie," Allie said, "what month is this?"

The boy gave Allie a funny look. "It's September, but—"

Allie grabbed Toby's shoulders. "You hear that, Toby?" she said. "It's September 1939! Max and Luna were going to October 1939. That means we only have to wait a month, and they'll show up right here!"

Ozzie held up one hand. "Hold it, hold it!" he said. "You are *really* blowing my mind! I didn't mean that this is the *year* 1939. I thought you were asking about the car over there. It's a 1939 Lincoln Continental. Are you telling me you don't even know what year this is?"

Allie shook her head. Toby, with his mouth open, just looked dumb.

"It's 1968!" Ozzie said. "Have you guys been on a bad trip or what?"

Allie's expression was bleak and disappointed. "Yeah," she said, "I guess you could call it a 'bad trip.'" She sat down on the curb and tried not to cry.

"Man, did you know you're breaking out in hives?" Ozzie asked.

"Not hives," Toby said. "Mosquito bites."

"That's a bad scene, man," Ozzie said. "We've got some calamine lotion in the house. Want me to get you some?"

"Yeah!" Toby snapped, scratching his arms. "And hurry up, will you? I'm about to scratch my skin off!"

"Toby," Allie said, "it wouldn't hurt you to say 'Please' and 'Thank you.'"

"Get off my back, O'Dell," Toby growled.

Ozzie went inside, then came out a few minutes later with a bottle of pink lotion and a handful of cotton balls. He handed the lotion and cotton to Allie. Toby sat down on the curb next to Allie, and she applied calamine lotion to Toby's face and arms.

"I'm leaving for school in twenty minutes," Ozzie said. "Do you guys need a lift? My dad can take us in the Lincoln."

"Well—" Allie hesitated. "I don't really know *what* to do."

Ozzie got down on one knee. "Sounds like you're in trouble."

Allie shrugged, dabbing at Toby's bites. "You can say that again. . . . Hold still, Toby! And stop scratching!"

"It itches!" Toby whined.

"What kind of trouble?" Ozzie asked.

"I—" Allie hesitated. "I'd rather not say."

Ozzie shrugged. "Okay," he said. "But if you want my dad to drive you into town—"

"Thanks," Allie said, "but I think we'd better stay here with the Volkswagen."

Ozzie looked around. "Volkswagen?" he said. "I don't see any Volkswagen."

Oops! Allie thought. "Uh—we sort of parked it in your backyard."

Ozzie blinked. "What's your Volkswagen doing in my backyard?"

"We, uh—" Allie winced a little. "We sort of got lost."

"You got lost—in my backyard?" Ozzie grinned. "Makes sense. Someone who doesn't know what year it is could get lost anywhere. Did your car break down or something?"

"Or something, yeah," Allie said.

"What a drag," Ozzie said. "Well, I'll have my dad take a look at it. He's an inventor. He's good at mechanical stuff."

"Oh, I don't want to bother him—," Allie protested.

"Hey, it's no hassle," Ozzie said. "My dad and I will meet you in the backyard, okay?"

Allie shrugged. "Okay," she said.

Ozzie dashed into the house.

Madame Hyde led Max and Luna to the atrium—a big court-yard in the middle of the building. "Young man," she said, turn-ing to Max, "you are about to see something that has no earthly explanation. Once you have seen it, I shall await your apology."

"Madame Hyde," Max said, "you might have a long wait."

The woman sniffed, then turned and began walking toward the far end of the atrium. The *clack-clack* of her footsteps echoed and re-echoed.

As the woman walked away, Luna felt a tingle of excite-ment inside her, as if she expected something wonderful to happen. Max, however, felt an inner alarm telling him that something terrible was about to happen.

The woman reached the center of the atrium floor and—

Whooosh! Searing clouds of flame erupted around her! Startled, Luna screamed and clutched Max's arm. The flames turned to smoke and hid Madame Hyde from view.

When the smoke cleared, Madame Hyde was gone.

Whooosh! Another billow of flame exploded to their right. Luna screamed again and clung more tightly to Max's arm—but this time, her scream was full of excitement, like a scream on a roller-coaster.

Whooosh! Another billow of flame exploded to their left.

"What do you think now, my doubting friend?" a voice echoed from the darkness above them—the voice of Madame Hyde.

Max looked up. The woman stood on the third-floor landing. She was balanced on the railing of the iron balustrade, with one hand gripping an iron post for support.

Luna gasped. "Max!" she said in an excited voice. "What's she going to do?"

Max glanced at Luna's profile, and saw that her face was alight with wonder. Suddenly, he felt sick inside. This demonstration, Max realized, was not just to convince him. It was also intended to make sure Luna had no doubts about Madame Hyde's power—and it was working.

Madame Hyde's voice rang out once more: "Guide my steps, O spirits fair / As I tread upon the air! / By your power, set me free / Of the curse of gravity! / As I will, so may it be!"

Wonder mingled with horror inside Luna as she watched Madame Hyde step off the railing. There was nothing between the woman's feet and the hard tiles of the atrium floor except forty feet of thin air.

Luna closed her eyes and screamed.

"Where are we?" Grady asked. He sat in the backseat of the hovercar behind the two Time Troopers. Looking out the clear bubble canopy, he saw nothing around him but a kaleidoscope of swirling colors.

"We are in a temporal vector," Trooper 7 said, "traveling outside of normal space and time."

"We are tracking your fellow time travelers," added Trooper 11, "by the trail of stray chronons emitted by their time machine."

"Chronons?" Grady said. "I think Max said something about chronons once. What are they?"

"Time particles," Trooper 11 said.

Grady nodded. "Tell me something—why are you chasing us?"

"You and your friends," Trooper 11 said, "have committed the crime of chronological trespass, in violation of the Temporal Security Act of 2099."

Grady frowned. "Sounds serious," he said.

"Quite serious," Trooper 7 replied.

Madame Hyde stepped off the iron railing and began to walk . . . on thin air.

Luna gasped. Max felt a sense of dread.

The raven-haired woman took one step, then another, then another, across sheer nothingness, as if she walked an invisible pathway through empty space. From below, Max looked for some telltale clue to explain the mystery. He saw nothing but what appeared to be a witch taking a stroll in the middle of the air.

"Woohoo!" Luna whooped, clapping and jumping. To Max, Luna was acting like a cheerleader—a cheerleader whose team was winning.

Moments later, Madame Hyde arrived at the other side of the atrium. She stepped lightly from the iron railing of the balustrade onto the third-floor landing. Then she waved her arms and—

Whooosh! She was once again swallowed up by billows of flame and smoke. As the smoke rose to the ceiling, Max and Luna saw that Madame Hyde had vanished once more.

It was a dazzling show, Max had to admit. But was it magic—or magick? Max had concluded that everything Madame Hyde said and did was some kind of lie.

Max glanced at Luna and saw the look of awe and wonder in her bright blue eyes. Clearly, the witch's lies were working on the girl.

Max and Luna waited in suspense for Madame Hyde to reappear. Seconds ticked by. Their tension mounted.

"Max," Luna said. "Where did she—"

Whooosh! Another billow of flame exploded directly in front of Max and Luna. The girl screamed and clutched

Max's arm. As the flame turned to smoke, and the smoke ascended toward the skylight—

Madame Hyde stood in front of them.

Luna jumped up and down excitedly. "Yes! Yes!" she said in a voice wild with greed—an intense, unquenchable greed for power. "That's what I want! That's what I came across time to get! Power! Real magickal power! Oh, Madame Hyde, I don't care if I ever get back to my own time, if only I can do the kind of magick you do!"

"You want power and knowledge," Madame Hyde said, "and you shall have it in abundance as my apprentice." She put her arm around Luna, then turned a fierce and mocking gaze on Max. "And you, dear boy—have you nothing to say after what you have seen?"

"You put on a good show," he said.

The woman's eyes narrowed dangerously. "Come, Luna," she said. "We have much to talk about, you and I."

Somewhere in the huge house of Madame Hyde, a clock chimed nine o'clock. Luna and Madame Hyde walked arm-in-arm toward the parlor. Max followed behind them, praying in silence.

6

THE DRAGON'S TALE

Allie and Toby went to the backyard and waited beside Timebender for Ozzie and his dad. Toby's face and arms were blotched and streaked with pink lotion that had begun to get dry and cakey. "I just realized something," Allie said glumly. "If we don't find a way out of 1968, we'll be in our mid-thirties by the time we're born."

"Huh?" Toby wrinkled his face.

"Never mind," Allie said. "Here they come."

Ozzie and his father came down the back steps of the house. They crossed the lawn toward the two time travelers and their Volkswagen. Mr. McCrane was a man in his mid-forties with thick brown hair and a touch of gray at the temples. Perched on his nose was a pair of round-lensed glasses—Allie was beginning to think those round glasses were a McCrane family trademark.

"Well, well," Ozzie's father said. "What have we here? A red-haired girl—and a pink-faced boy."

"Ha-ha," Toby said. "Very funny."

Allie nudged him in the shin—hard.

"Ow!" Toby winced.

"Be nice," she said. "We need his help."

"Dad," Ozzie said, "meet Allie and Toby."

"Hi, Allie. Hi, Toby," said Mr. McCrane. "I'm Horton McCrane."

"Nice to meet you," Allie said. "Sorry about parking on your grass."

"Well, no harm done," Mr. McCrane said. He walked around the car. "What's wrong with your car? Out of gas?"

Allie shook her head. "I don't think so."

Mr. McCrane lifted the engine cover at the rear of the car. Where the engine should have been was just an empty hole. "Well," Horton McCrane said, "I think I found your problem. No engine."

"Really?" Allie said, taking a look. "Well, what do you know?"

"Yeah," Mr. McCrane said, slamming the engine cover down. "I wonder how you got this car into my backyard without an engine. Want to try explaining it?"

"I'd rather not," she said.

"How about you, Toby?" Mr. McCrane asked. "Care to explain?"

Toby shrugged. "We came here in a time machine," he said.

Horton McCrane chuckled. "Wise guy, huh? Okay, you don't have to tell me if you don't want to." He looked from Allie's unhappy face to Toby's pink, pasty face. "Looks like you two are in some kind of trouble. Running away from home? Or from the police?"

"Oh, no!" Allie said. "Nothing like that! It's just—well, it's complicated."

"All right," said Horton McCrane. "How can I help you?"

Allie thought for a moment. "Do you know anything about quantum physics?" she asked. "It's a matter of life and death."

Mr. McCrane looked surprised. "A quantum physics emergency, eh? Subatomic particles and quantum space-time and that sort of thing? Well, I know a *little* about it— but my field is engineering, not physics. You need to see Professor Werner Von Plonck. He's head of the Physics Department at the university."

"Dad teaches part-time in the Engineering Department," Ozzie added, "when he's not working on inventions."

Mr. McCrane checked his watch. "I have to take Oswald to school, and then I'm going to the university myself. I'll take you there and you can talk to the professor."

"That would be great!" Allie said.

"What about your car?" Mr. McCrane asked. "I've got

a tow chain in the Lincoln. We could tow it to a service station."

"Could you tow it to the university, instead?" Allie asked. "Our physics problem has to do with Timeben—I mean, with the Volkswagen."

Horton McCrane scratched his head. "A quantum Beetle, eh? Sure, I can tow it to the university, if you want. But we'd better get going or Oswald will be late for school."

Minutes later, he brought the Lincoln down a side road and through the walnut grove. He backed the big car up to the Volkswagen and attached the tow chain. Then they all got in the Lincoln—Ozzie and his dad in front, Allie and Toby in back. They drove off toward town with the battered orange time machine trailing behind them.

Madame Hyde led Max and Luna back to the crystal parlor. They found Mr. Woothering waiting stiffly at the door to the parlor. "Woothering," Madame Hyde said, "some refreshments for our guests."

"Yes, Madame," Mr. Woothering said. He turned and left.

They went inside and sat down together at the table once more.

"So, young man," Madame Hyde said, "you are not impressed."

"Oh, I'm impressed, all right," Max said. "I like a good magic act."

"Oh, Max!" Luna said, glaring at him. "You are so thick-headed! When Madame Hyde walked on air, that was *more* than magick! It was a *miracle!*"

"No!" Max said. "Don't ever confuse magick with miracles. A miracle is something only God can do. A miracle isn't a lot of flash and fire and noise. A miracle is when God surprises you and reaches into your life and changes you! I've seen miracles—*real* miracles. And what Madame Hyde did out there was no miracle."

Luna shook her head. "You're hopeless."

"I don't like lies," Max said. "And Madame Hyde has been lying to you big-time. Look, Luna, every stage magician uses something called 'misdirection' to make an illusion seem real. And Madame Hyde uses a lot of misdirection. Didn't you notice all the distractions that were going on? *Boom!* There's a big explosion on our left! And *zap!*—Madame Hyde pops up on our right. That's nothing but plain old stage magic."

"How clever you are!" Madame Hyde said with a superior smile. "You talk about misdirection—yet you use misdirection yourself."

"What do you mean?" Max asked.

"Isn't it obvious?" Madame Hyde said. "You accuse me of deception in order to cover your own lies."

"I didn't—"

"Earlier this evening," the woman said, "you claimed you time-traveled to the Garden of Eden—and you offered no proof whatsoever. And now you brazenly accuse me of deception—again, without proof—even though I demonstrated my powers right before your eyes. You accuse me of fraud. I submit that the only fraud here is *you*. I think Luna can see who is lying and who is telling the truth."

"I sure can," Luna said, glaring at Max.

Max fought down a rising feeling of anger. "Madame Hyde," he said, "you claim you use real witchcraft to walk on air, right? Well, fine. Maybe you do. But if that's true, then that would make you a servant of the serpent—the Dragon—I met in the Garden of Eden, and a servant of evil."

Madame Hyde threw her head back and laughed. "Oh, so you claim to have met the Dragon!"

"That's right," Max said. "And like you, he's very clever at making good look bad and bad look good. You and the Dragon are a lot alike."

"I'm flattered," Madame Hyde said. "I am indeed a servant of the Dragon of Eden." Unthinkingly, she reached up and rubbed a spot in the middle of her forehead. "The Dragon is the source of my power."

"I thought so," Max said. He turned to the girl. "Luna," he said, "you don't understand what you are playing around with. The power that the Dragon gives is never free. There are always strings attached. No, not strings—

chains. He lures you in, gives you all kinds of bright and shiny pleasures, makes all kinds of smooth promises. He takes you in gradually, so gradually you don't even know it's happening. After a while, everything that was bright and shiny turns dark and ugly. And then it's too late to back out—and the Dragon has you right where he wants you."

"Max," Luna said, "how can you be so smart and so stupid at the same time? Madame Hyde uses magick to do good. No matter where the power comes from, we witches control the results. You heard that phrase in Madame Hyde's spell? 'As I will, so may it be.' That's an ancient formula for binding the spirits to do our will. If our intentions are good, then even *evil* spirits must use their power to do good."

"Oh, man!" Max squinched his eyes shut in frustration. "Luna, that's so wrong! You can't mix Light and Darkness! The power of magick comes from the Darkness, and it only does what the Darkness wants. You think you can bind evil spirits to your will? Eventually, they bind you to do theirs! You can't do good things with bad power."

"But the Dragon—," Luna said.

"The Dragon disguises himself as an angel of light—but he's still a demon, straight from the Darkness. If you mess around with magick, you'll end up in Darkness forever."

Just then, Woothering returned with a tray of refreshments—some tea, fruit, crackers, and cheese. He set the tray on the table and served Luna, then Max, then Madame

Hyde. Once everyone was served, he turned and left the parlor.

"Max," Luna said, "you just don't understand what witchcraft is all about. You think I just want power, but that's not true. I also want *wisdom*—the ancient wisdom for controlling spirits and forces, and using their power to do good."

"The only real wisdom is knowing God," Max said. "Your 'wisdom' is a lie—like the original lie the Dragon told Adam and Eve. The Dragon told them that if they did what God had forbidden, they would be as gods. Isn't that what you want? Magickal power—the power to be your own god? Luna, you're falling for the oldest trick in the book."

"But the white magick—"

"White magick, black magick, it's all the same, Luna. God hates it, because all magick comes from the Dragon, from wanting to be equal to God, from putting your will above His will."

Madame Hyde smirked. "A lovely speech," she said. "But you tell only one side of the story. What about the Dragon's side of the story?"

"Huh?" Max said. "What do you mean?"

The woman rose from her chair and went over to a bookcase that contained dozens of old books. Max squinted through his glasses at the titles: *Pagan Lore*, *The Art and Science of Crystal Gazing*, *The Philosophy of Witchcraft*, *Practical Magick*, *The Necronimicon*, *The Chronicles of Merlin*, *The Book of Shadows,* and more.

Then Max saw the book Madame Hyde was reaching for: *The Testament of the Silver Dragon.*

The book was bound in reptile leather, and the title was stamped in silver. Madame Hyde brought it back to the table and offered it to Max, but he refused to touch it. She handed it to Luna.

"May I take it over there," Luna said, "where the light is better?"

"Please do," said Madame Hyde.

Luna got up and carried the book over by the fireplace.

Madame Hyde leaned toward Max. "That book," she said, "tells how the Dragon went to Adam and Eve and offered them knowledge and power—the hidden knowledge that would make them as gods. When the Dragon urged the woman to try the fruit that had been forbidden by their Maker, he wasn't trying to trick them. He wanted them to know true wisdom. But the Maker wanted to keep Adam and Eve in ignorance. He wanted them to worship only Him. He didn't want them to know that they, too, could be as gods, and that they could worship anyone or anything they chose—even themselves."

"I've heard all of this before," Max said, "but not out of some musty old book. I heard it right from the Dragon's mouth. It's nothing but lies."

"I feel sorry for you, young man," the woman said. "Your religion is filled with silly rules. 'Thou shalt not do this' and 'Thou shalt not do that.' How sad for you."

Max laughed. "Why? Because God has given me guidelines for a happy life?"

"You don't know what you're missing, dear boy," the woman said. "You've never felt the energy of the Dragon surging through you. Look around you! Look at all the wealth that is mine. Look at this beautiful house I live in. All this is mine because of the power I have as a witch and a priestess of the Old Religion."

"I don't want your kind of power," Max said. "God has the power and wisdom to make the universe. When my body dies, I'll still have my eternal soul. But when you die—"

"Enough!" Madame Hyde snapped, covering her ears. "I won't listen to any more of your myths and fables. Luna, dear, have you been listening to this nonsense?"

Luna didn't answer.

"Luna—?" the woman said, turning around. The leather-bound book lay on the floor in front of the fireplace, along with Luna's purse. But Luna herself was gone.

"Where did she go?" Max asked. "I didn't see her leave!"

In the corner, the clock began chiming ten.

Madame Hyde put her hand to her mouth. "Oh, no!" she said. "Come with me!" She jumped up and hurried out of the room with Max close behind her.

"Allie," Horton McCrane said over his shoulder as he drove, "where do you and Toby go to school?"

"Victor Appleton Middle School," Allie said.

Ozzie McCrane turned around and gave Allie and Toby a puzzled look. "What's a 'middle school'?"

"A middle school," Allie said, "is like a junior high, except that a middle school only has seventh and eighth grades. When you hit ninth grade, you go to high school."

"Oh, right," Ozzie said. "At Debockel Junior High, we have seventh through ninth grades."

"Allie," Mr. McCrane said, "I'm sure I know all the schools in this town—but I've never heard of Victor Appleton Middle School."

Ooops, Allie thought, suddenly remembering that Victor Appleton Middle School was built in the late 1980s. She didn't want to lie—but if she told the truth, it would *sound* like a lie: You see, Mr. McCrane, we're from the twenty-first century, and the school we go to doesn't even exist in 1968. How would *that* sound? Allie was trying to think of an answer when—

"We go to school a long time from here," Toby said.

Horton McCrane looked baffled. "Do you mean," he said, "it takes a long time to get to your school?"

"Yeah," Toby said. "That, too."

Allie looked at Toby, then grinned. Considering the situation they were in, it wasn't a bad answer. And it wasn't a lie.

Mr. McCrane puzzled a moment over that answer, then

he shrugged. Allie was afraid he was about to ask another question—but then she saw the front fence of Debockel Junior High School. Mr. McCrane stopped the car at the curb. Ozzie jumped out, waved good-bye, and joined the crowd of people streaming into the halls. Mr. McCrane put the car in gear and pulled away from the curb.

"Is it far to the university?" Allie asked.

"Not far," Mr. McCrane said. "We'll be there in three or four minutes."

The Time Troopers arrived in the backyard of the McCrane House on a September morning in 1968. The hovercar floated motionless at treetop level. "They were here," Time Trooper 11 said. "The chronon traces are strong."

Seated behind the robots, Grady said, "Maybe they timebended."

"No," Trooper 11 said. "The trail of time particles leads that way, toward the town."

"Let's go," Trooper 7 said. "It won't be hard to track them."

The black-and-white hovercar sailed over the walnut grove and flew toward town.

Madame Hyde and Max McCrane ran to the atrium. Max looked all around, but didn't see Luna anywhere. Then he heard Madame Hyde gasp.

"Look!" the woman said in a strangled voice.

Max looked up. Luna stood on the railing of the third-floor landing. Her platinum-gold hair seemed to glow in the darkness.

"Luna, no!" shouted Madame Hyde. "You don't know what you're doing!"

"I know the spell," Luna called back, her voice echoing. "I can do this!"

"Luna, don't move!" Max shouted. "I'm coming up the stairs!" He dashed to the foot of the staircase.

"Don't, Max!" Luna commanded. "I don't want an unbelieving cowan near me when I do this!"

Max hesitated.

"Luna, don't!" Madame Hyde said. "You're not ready!"

But Luna ignored the woman's plea. In a clear, loud voice, she said, "Guide my steps, O spirits fair / As I tread upon the air! / By your power, set me free / Of the curse of gravity! / As I will, so may it be!"

As Max watched helplessly, Luna let go of the iron support post and took a step off the railing.

7

"Don't Let Go!"

Luna expected her foot to come down on something firm—
a magickal, invisible pathway through the air. She was
absolutely astonished when her foot simply sank into
empty space.

She was actually *falling!*

Her arms flailed—

Her right hand struck something—

Held on—

Hard iron dug into her fingers and the palm of her hand.

The muscles of her right arm were jerked taut, like a
tightly stretched rope being suddenly twanged. Needles of
pain pierced her arm—but she had stopped falling.

She was holding on to the ornamental ironwork of the
third-floor balustrade by her right hand. Looking between
her dangling feet, she saw the marble floor three stories

down. She tried to scream but could only manage a strangled whimper.

The fingers of her right hand screamed with pain. She tried to reach up with her left hand, but the effort sent lightning bolts of pain through her right shoulder.

"Max!" she wailed.

"Coming!" Max answered from somewhere below, his voice and pounding footsteps echoing through the atrium. "Hold on!"

Luna knew she wasn't going to make it. Her fingers were already slipping. Her strength was giving out. The pain was already unbearable.

It would be so easy to let go. . . .

⊚ ⊚ ⊚

On the way to the university, Mr. McCrane drove past the old Royal Theatre. Looking out the side window of the Lincoln, Allie read the big marquee:

NOW SHOWING:
2001: A SPACE ODYSSEY
THE ULTIMATE TRIP!

That reminded Allie of the good times, before her mom and dad's divorce. Her dad had rented *2001: A Space Odyssey* on DVD, and he had coaxed Allie and her mom to watch it with him. "Best movie ever made!" he'd said. Turned out, it was a long, slow, boring movie—no starship battles or funny robots, but plenty of dull classical music. Allie and her mom both fell asleep halfway through. Allie's dad had been grumpy all the next day because—as he put it—"you slept through all the good stuff." *There was "good stuff"?*

Allie's thoughts were still on missing her mom and dad when Mr. McCrane's black Lincoln pulled into the university parking lot. Mr. McCrane found two empty parking spaces in a row, and he parked so that the Lincoln was in one space and the Volkswagen in the other. He got out and unhooked the tow chain while Toby stood and strapped on his backpack. Allie went to the Volkswagen and retrieved Max's notebook, placing it in her purse.

Mr. McCrane tossed the chain in the trunk of his car and brushed off his hands. "Well, Allie and Toby," he said, "I sure hope everything works out for you."

"Thanks for your help," Allie said.

"There's the Science Building," Mr. McCrane said, pointing. "Professor Von Plonck's office is on the second floor." He checked his watch. "My class starts in ten minutes—got to go!" With a smile and a wave, he left.

Allie turned to Toby. "Stop scratching!" she said. "The calamine lotion won't work if you rub it all off."

"Dude!" Toby said. "It itches! I don't think that pink gunk works at all!"

Allie looked him up and down. His clothes were dirty and grass-stained, and his arms and face were caked with a bright pink crust. "You're a mess," she said. "Well, come on. Let's go find the professor."

It had only been a few seconds, but Luna felt like she'd been holding on to the ironwork for ages. She could hear Max's footsteps running up the stairs—but she knew he was going to be too late. "I can't hold on, Max!" she whimpered.

With that, her fingers slipped from the ironwork. Luna shut her eyes and screamed—

Miraculously, she didn't fall.

Luna opened her eyes—and saw Max! His face was pressed against a gap in the ornamental ironwork. His glasses were askew. He had shoved both hands through a gap in the ironwork. He was gripping her right wrist with all his might.

"Max!" Luna said. "Pull me up!"

Max's face was turning red. "Can't!" was all he could say.

Luna felt her arm slipping through Max's grasp. "Tighter, Max!" she said. She felt his hands clamp her arm a little tighter—but she knew he couldn't hold on forever.

She felt the blood pounding in her brain. Her vision was swimming. She thought she would black out—

Then two more faces appeared over the railing: Madame

Hyde and Mr. Woothering. "Reach up with your other hand, dear!" Madame Hyde called.

Luna raised her left arm, trembling with fear and strain.

Mr. Woothering reached down and grasped her hand. Luna was surprised that an old man like Mr. Woothering had such a strong grip. She felt herself being lifted up, up, over the railing. Mr. Woothering had her in his arms.

"Woothering," Madame Hyde said, "carry her to the sofa in the parlor."

"Yes, Madame," Mr. Woothering said. He turned and gently carried Luna down the staircase.

"And you, young man," Madame Hyde said, turning to Max. "I owe you a debt of gratitude. How horrible if the poor girl had died just now!"

"I don't want your gratitude," Max said angrily. "You've got Luna believing all that stuff about magick spells and witchcraft. If she'd been killed tonight, it would have been your fault!"

Madame Hyde's face hardened and her eyes smoldered. "What Luna chooses to believe is none of your concern." She paused. "And why don't you try doing something useful—like figuring out a way to get back to your own time? I assure you, young man, you are *not* welcome in mine."

Madame Hyde turned her back on Max and continued down the stairs. Her footsteps echoed hollowly through the atrium.

Max stood watching her, his body shaking. He took one last look around the atrium and was about to go downstairs—but then he did a double take. He leaned against the balustrade, peering up toward the skylight. He smiled and nodded to himself, then hurried down the staircase.

◎ ◎ ◎

Allie and Toby stopped in front of Professor Von Plonck's office door.

"Look, Toby," she said, "the professor may be our only hope. So try not to be a brat, okay?"

"Drop dead," Toby said.

Allie sighed. "Thanks, Toby, I knew I could count on you." She turned and knocked on the door.

"Come in," said a voice inside.

Allie and Toby went inside and found the professor sitting behind a messy desk. Papers and books were stacked everywhere. The books had titles like *Matrix Mechanics in Quantum Theory*, *Cosmology and Space-time Structure*, and *Quantum Logic*. The professor looked at them over his wire-rimmed glasses. "Yes?" he said.

Professor Von Plonck wore a rumpled white shirt, a rumpled black suit, and a narrow black tie. He had a pointed chin and a bulging dome of a forehead—as if his brain was almost too big for his head. His black hair was wild and uncombed, and his black eyebrows were bushy.

"Professor," Allie said, approaching the desk, "I'm Allie O'Dell, and this is Toby Brubaker. We need your help."

"Oh?" said the professor. "What kind of help?"

"Can you tell us what this means?" Allie took Max's notebook from her purse and handed it to the professor.

Professor Von Plonck examined Max's calculations—and he blinked. Then he blinked again. "Oh, my!" he said.

"What is it, Professor?" Allie asked.

The professor pointed to the notebook. "See this variable here?" he said. "That represents the attenuation of a light signal as it is being transduced through a fourth-dimensional structure. This symbol here represents the speed of light, and these represent the coherent factor, the elevation displacement, and the degree of polarization. If I'm not mistaken, this is some sort of worksheet for calculating the rate, direction, and range of transmission in four-dimensional space-time—correct?"

Allie shrugged. "I only know that it has something to do with time travel."

"Aha!" The professor's face lit up. "I thought so! Let's see, if we were to use this variable here to represent years, and these to represent days and hours—But what are these variables here? Oh, yes. Coordinates on a geoidal surface. Ah! Very sophisticated calculations! I'd like to meet the man responsible for this work!"

"Actually," Allie said, "a *boy* did those calculations."

The professor pointed to Toby. "Not *this* boy!"

"Of course not," Allie said. "It was a boy named Max." She paused. "I'd better start at the beginning. You see, Toby and I are from the future—the twenty-first century."

The professor's bushy eyebrows went up.

"And my friend Max," Allie continued, "who's also from the future, invented a time machine called Timebender. Max and a girl named Luna got lost in 1939, so Toby and a guy named Grady and I took Timebender and went looking for them. We took a wrong turn into the future, and then we went back to the Pleistocene Epoch, and Toby almost got smashed by a woolly mammoth, and Grady got left behind, and I think the Time Troopers may be coming after us and—"

"Hold it, young lady," the professor said. "Stop and take a breath!"

Allie took a breath.

"I understand everything," the professor continued.

Allie's jaw dropped. "You do?"

"Absolutely," the professor said.

"Cool!" Allie said. "What do we do?"

"First," the professor said, "go back to Dr. Schmutz and tell him, 'Nice try.'"

Allie looked baffled. "Huh?"

"Tell him his little prank didn't work," said the professor. "Oh, I admit he had me going there with those calculations, but does Dr. Schmutz think he can fool me with this ridiculous story about a boy inventing a time machine?

Everyone knows time travel is impossible! Now, if you'll excuse me, I'm very busy—"

"But it's not a joke!" Allie said. "We are from the future!"

"Of course you are," Professor Von Plonck said with a grin, "and I'm the Mad Hatter and you're Alice and your friend here is the White Rabbit and this is Wonderland. Now, if you would kindly step through that looking glass and let me return to my work—"

"All right, all right," Allie said. "Let's go, Toby."

The hovercar floated into the university parking lot. "The trail of time particles is fading," Trooper 11 said. "It leads to this vehicle storage zone—then stops."

"The humans call a vehicle storage zone a 'parking lot,'" Trooper 7 said.

"There must be a hundred Volkswagens here," Grady said.

"There are exactly seventy-three Volkswagen vehicles here," Trooper 7 replied. "Of those seventy-three Volkswagens, sixteen are coated in a paint that reflects light in a range from 5,970 to 6,220 angstroms."

"I don't get this 'angstrom' stuff," Grady said.

"I mean," Trooper 7 said, "that there are sixteen Volkswagens in the color range you call 'orange.'"

"Oh," Grady said—then he did a double take. He spotted

Timebender. It was dented and bashed, just as he had last seen it. Grady felt a surge of hope: *If Timebender is here, then Allie and Toby must be nearby!*

As the hovercar passed within a few feet of Timebender, Grady noticed a stranger crouching next to the VW. Was he trying to break in? No, he was *painting* Timebender! He had long black hair and a beard, and he wore beads around his neck and sandals on his feet. He had a box with dozens of spray cans, and he was spray-painting bright, colorful flowers and butterflies onto the VW. He painted swiftly in broad splashes of color. As Grady watched, the stranger finished decorating one side of the car and moved quickly to the other side.

Grady glanced at the Time Troopers—and saw that they were looking right at Timebender! "That one looks similar to the suspect vehicle," Trooper 11 said, pointing. "The spectrometer indicates a probable color match."

"But the body configuration is wrong," Trooper 7 said. "The suspect vehicle was not damaged."

Grady was amazed—the Troopers passed right by Timebender, the very "suspect vehicle" they were looking for! Timebender was right under their stainless-steel noses—and they didn't know it! Then Grady remembered that the Troopers had seen Timebender before it had been bashed by a bull mammoth!

"Continue scanning," said Trooper 7. "The fugitives and their vehicle must be nearby."

Allie and Toby left Professor Von Plonck's office. Allie choked back a big lump in her throat. *I'm not going to let Toby see me cry!* she told herself.

As they walked down the stairs of the Science Building, Allie prayed, *God, I'm so scared! Max and Luna are lost in 1939, and Grady is back there with the mammoths and saber-toothed cats! Everything I try just makes things worse! God, please show me what to do!*

"What do we do now?" Toby asked as they reached the bottom of the stairs.

"We go back to the car," Allie said. "I need to think things over."

They walked out of the Science Building and headed for the parking lot. Halfway across the lot, Toby stopped in his tracks. "Dude!" he said. "Stubblefield can't be lost!"

Allie looked at Toby. "What do you mean?"

"Think about it," Toby said. "You were in McCrane's backyard when the Beetle popped up out of nowhere, right?"

"Yeah," Allie said. "And stop scratching."

"Who jumped out of the car?"

"You, me, and—" Allie gasped. "Oh, wow! Grady was in that VW, too! So if we were seeing our own future, that means we *will* find Grady again!"

"Yeah," Toby said, gulping hard. "But it also means that those Time-Dorks will be chasing us."

Allie's heart sank. "Oh, yeah." She paused, thinking it over. "Well, there's nothing we can do about that. We'll just have to face the future when it gets here. Come on."

They continued through the parking lot until they got to Timebender—then they stopped and stared in disbelief.

"Dude!" Toby said.

"Oh, no!" Allie said. "It's like a bad dream coming true!"

Someone had painted bright, colorful designs all over Timebender: rainbows, butterflies, white doves, and flowers—lots and lots of flowers. Along the rear fender, the words FLOWER POWER appeared in bright blue paint.

A stranger popped up behind the Volkswagen. Allie jumped. Toby yelled, "Aaaagh!"

"Hey, man!" said the stranger, coming around the car. "Don't freak! I didn't mean to trip you out!"

The stranger had a dark beard and mustache, and long dark hair bound by a headband.

He wore a colorful paisley shirt, a flowered vest, faded bell-bottom denims, leather sandals, and two strands of colorful beads around his neck. There was a can of spray paint in his hand and a box of spray cans at his feet.

Allie stepped closer, looking at the stranger and his artwork. "Why did you paint our car?" Allie asked.

"Because it looked so sad, all bashed up and dented," the stranger said. "I made it happy—see? Is that out of sight or what?"

"But it wasn't your car!" Allie said. "You had no right—"

"Dude!" Toby interrupted, staring at the stranger. "Are you a hippie?"

"'Hippie' is just a label, man," the stranger replied. "You look at me and call me 'hippie.' What if I looked at you, with all that stuff on your face, and called you 'pinkie'? The way I see it, we're all just people. If we wouldn't label each other, there'd be no war, no hate. The world would be beautiful! . . . You guys got any bread?"

"Bread?" Allie asked, confused. "You mean, like, to make a sandwich?"

"No," the hippie said, "I mean folding green, mazuma— uh, whadduyahcallit—money."

"I get it," Toby said. "The hippie wants a handout."

"No way!" the hippie said. "I'm an artist, and I just performed a service for you fine people. I turned that orange eyesore into a mind-blowing work of art! Now, I don't want to be *paid*—that would be capitalism! But I do accept donations—say, five bucks?"

"But we didn't want our car painted!" Allie said.

"Now that it's done," the hippie said, "you've got to admit, it's really groovy."

Allie took another look at the decorated Volkswagen. She shrugged. "Well," she said, "I guess 'groovy' is in the eye of the beholder."

"See?" said the hippie. "I knew you'd dig it. Now, about that donation—"

Allie reached into her purse and pulled out a five-dollar

bill. The hippie took it, glanced at it—then looked at it again. "Whoa! Freaky money!" He held up the bill. "Where'd you get this trippy bread, little lady?"

Allie looked at the bill. It was one of the new-style bills with an enlarged picture of Abraham Lincoln on it. It was dated 2002. It looked *way* different from 1968 money.

"I'm sorry," Allie said. "I guess this money isn't any good here."

The hippie folded the money and stuck it in his shirt pocket. "No sweat," he said. "I'll keep it as a conversation piece. I'll say it came here by time machine!" He laughed.

Allie and Toby looked at each other and shrugged.

"Well," the hippie said, "thanks for the donation, uh— What are your names?"

Allie said, "I'm Allie and this is Toby."

"Far out," said the hippie, shaking their hands. "My name's Dakota—Dakota Skyes. People call me Dak."

"Your last name is Skyes?" Toby said. "Are you related to—"

"Toby! This is 1968—Luna isn't even born yet."

"Oh, yeah," Toby said. "Never mind."

Dakota looked from Allie to Toby—then he shrugged. "You two are on a really heavy trip! I can't—" He stopped, rubbed his eyes, and stared strangely. "Far out! I'm having a psychedelic experience!"

Allie looked puzzled. "You're having a *what?*"

"I'm seeing visions," Dakota said. "A freaky car that floats. And inside the car, I see fuzz with metal faces. Whoa, this is no vision! The metal fuzz are coming this way! I'm out of here!" He made a *V* sign with two fingers.

"Peace!" he said, then he picked up his box of paints and hurried away.

"'The metal fuzz are coming'?" Allie asked. "What did he mean by that?"

Toby turned and his eyes widened. "I think he means *them!*" Toby groaned.

A black-and-white hovercar was cruising the parking lot just two rows over. Allie grabbed Toby by the shirt and dragged him behind Timebender.

"This can't be happening," Toby groaned.

"Hey!" Allie whispered. "Don't lean against the car! That's wet paint!"

Too late. Toby had blue paint on his hands and a bright yellow smear on his backpack. "Why didn't you tell me *before* I leaned against it?"

"Shh!" Allie said. "Hear that?"

It was a humming sound—the sound of the hovercar. It was growing louder.

The Time Troopers were coming.

8

SPOONBENDER

Mr. Woothering set Luna down on the sofa across from the fireplace. Madame Hyde arranged some satin pillows under Luna's head. "There, there, poor thing. You've had a terrible ordeal."

"Why?" Luna whimpered. "I said the spell correctly. I *believed* in it. Why didn't it work?" She rubbed her shoulder, wincing in pain.

Max entered the parlor and stood over Luna. "Are you all right?" he asked.

"I don't know," the girl said weakly. "I think so."

"Woothering," said Madame Hyde, "bring some tea. Quickly."

"Yes, Madame." Woothering departed at once.

Madame Hyde turned to the girl on the sofa. "Luna, dear, you must understand that the magickal arts are not mastered in a day. You start by learning to levitate a few inches off the ground—not by walking off a third-floor railing! I didn't attempt walking on air until I had practiced the craft for years—"

"You should mention, Madame Hyde," Max interrupted, "that you do it with the help of wires and a safety harness."

The woman whirled on Max, her face red with fury. "Liar!" she snapped.

Max said nothing. He felt no need to defend himself—the truth was on his side.

Luna sat up on the sofa, wincing. "Max," she said, "what are you saying?"

"There's a track in the ceiling," Max said. "It runs along the skylight. You can't see it unless you're up on the third floor."

"You don't know what you saw," Madame Hyde said.

"Thin steel wire," Max said, "the kind they use to make people fly around in stage shows, is invisible from three floors down, especially when the lighting isn't good. And big fiery explosions create a distraction and dazzle the eyes. I imagine Mr. Woothering was in charge of the fire effects."

"An imaginative theory, young man," Madame Hyde said bitterly.

"This woman is such a fake," Max said. "Luna, aren't you beginning to see that?"

Madame Hyde started to say something—then she clamped her mouth shut and glared at Max in a cold rage.

Luna settled back on the sofa. "I—I don't know what to believe."

Minutes passed in uncomfortable silence.

Finally, Mr. Woothering returned with a silver tea tray. He set the tray down on the table.

"Serve Luna first," Madame Hyde said. "One lump or two, dear?"

"One, please," Luna said.

Woothering used small silver tongs to place a lump of sugar in a china cup, then he poured the tea and stirred it with a silver spoon. As Luna sat up on the sofa, Woothering placed the teacup and saucer in her hands.

"Thank you," Luna said.

"Tea, sir?" Mr. Woothering said.

"No, thanks," Max said—then, "Wait! Yes, please. One lump. And leave me the spoon, please."

Max sat down at the table and Mr. Woothering placed the teacup, saucer, and spoon in front of him. Max picked up the spoon and stirred the tea—then he paused, holding the spoon up in front of him.

"Luna," he said, "you want me to teach you some *real* magic?"

"What?" Luna said. "You don't know anything about magick."

"Watch," Max said, standing up from the table. Carrying the silver teaspoon in both hands, he went over to the sofa and knelt beside Luna. "Here," he said. "You hold the handle of the spoon. That way you can tell I'm not using physical force on it."

Luna shrugged. "Okay," she said. She grasped the handle while Max held the upper part of the spoon. Max passed his right hand back and forth over the bowl of the spoon.

Madame Hyde crept forward, peering over Max's shoulder.

"With the power of my mind," Max said, "I command this spoon to bend! . . . bend! . . . *bend!*"

And as Luna, Madame Hyde, and Mr. Woothering looked on, the spoon began to bend—*all by itself!*

Madame Hyde snatched the spoon from Max and Luna, and stared at it. The spoon was bent at a 30-degree angle. "But," she sputtered, "that's *impossible!* It's a *trick!*"

"Madame Hyde," Max said with a chuckle, "are you calling me a *fake?* Are you telling me that you—a practicing *witch*—are a skeptic?"

Madame Hyde glared at Max. "How did you do that?"

Crouched behind Timebender, Allie and Toby heard the hum of the approaching hovercar. "They found us!" Toby panted.

"Don't panic!" Allie whispered.

"I'm not panicking!" Toby wailed, his voice rising to a pig-squeal.

The hum was very loud. The air felt charged with electricity. The Time Troopers were close. Allie turned to tell Toby not to move—

Toby was gone.

She looked around frantically—then she saw Toby running across the parking lot, toward the street. *He left me!* Allie thought. *He left me all alone!* Without thinking, she stood up and watched Toby dash away.

"Do not move!" an electronic voice thundered.

Allie jumped. The Time Troopers' hovercar was right in front of her. Inside the bubble canopy, the two Troopers glared at her with electronic eyes. And behind them—

"*Grady!*" Allie screamed. She was so glad to see him, she almost forgot about the Time Troopers.

Grady shouted to her. She couldn't hear Grady's voice through the bubble canopy, but she could read his lips: "Run, Allie, run!"

Allie turned and ran through the parking lot. In front of her were the buildings and tree-lined lawns of the university campus. Behind her, she heard the approaching hum of the Time Troopers' hovercar.

Allie dashed out of the parking lot and onto a sidewalk that led through the campus. People stopped and looked as Allie ran past; others stared toward the parking lot. A strange black-and-white vehicle was approaching—and it was floating three feet off the ground! Someone screamed. The crowd scattered in all directions.

Allie's feet pounded the sidewalk in time with the pounding of her heart. *How did the Time Troopers track us here?* she wondered as she ran. Then she remembered the sight of Grady sitting in the hovercar, behind the Troopers. Suddenly, her joy overcame her terror. *Grady's here!* she prayed as she ran. *Thank You, God!*

Max doubled over, laughing uncontrollably. "I shouldn't laugh, but the looks on your faces are funny! You want to know how spoon-bending works? It's simple: You bend the spoon when no one's looking!"

"What?" Luna and Madame Hyde said together.

"It's a trick I learned from my dad," Max said. "He knows all kinds of tricks and illusions."

"But I *saw* the spoon bend with my own eyes!" Luna said.

"That's what's so cool about spoon-bending!" Max said. "It's a simple trick, but it fools people every time. You just have to make sure people are looking somewhere else when you bend the spoon. Remember, I was talking to you while I took the spoon off the table. You were distracted while I brought the spoon behind the table for half a second. That half a second was when I bent it. When I brought the spoon over to you, Luna, I held it in both hands. Why? To keep you from seeing that it was *already bent*. I even let you hold the handle so you'd think the spoon was under your control."

"But I *know* what I saw!" Luna said. "I *saw* it bend!"

"You *think* you saw it bend," Max said. "While I moved my right hand back and forth over the spoon, my left hand moved down the bend in the spoon. It looked like the spoon was bending, but I was only *revealing* the bend I had already made."

Luna shook her head slowly. "It was just a trick. It looked so real—"

"That's what deception is all about," Max said. He stood up and walked away from the sofa.

"Where are you going?" Madame Hyde asked.

"I have another trick to show Luna," Max said. He passed the table in the middle of the room, then paused. The paperback copy of *The Wisdom of Witchdom* sat on the table where Madame Hyde had left it, next to the crystal ball. Max picked up the book and gave it a light toss. It landed with a smack on the carpet between the fireplace and the red velvet sofa where Luna rested.

"After I show you *this* trick, Luna," Max said, "you probably won't have such a high opinion of that book—or its author." Then he turned his steps toward the open doorway leading to the atrium.

"Woothering—!" Madame Hyde whispered.

"Yes, Madame," Woothering said. He moved toward Max—but he was too late.

Max stood beside the doorway and waved his arms. "Abracadabra, alakazam! Snuff out the candles, zippity-zam!" Instantly, all the candles in the parlor went out. So did the flames in the fireplace. Max waved his arms again. "Abracadabra, alakazee! Light those candles, one-two-*three!*" The candles and fireplace lit up again.

Madame Hyde howled in rage.

Woothering grabbed Max's arms. "Stop that right now!" he shouted.

"I think I made my point," Max said, shrugging out of the old man's grasp.

Max walked over to where Luna sat wide-eyed on the sofa. "You see, Luna?" He pointed to the marble tile floor. "I noticed where Madame Hyde stood when she did that candle trick—right next to the doorway. One tile by the door is darker than the rest. That's the button. The 'candles' aren't really candles at all—just gas jets. Press the tile with your heel and presto! The candles go on or off."

"It's all a fake!" Luna said in a tragic voice.

"Luna—," Madame Hyde said.

"I *believed* in you," Luna said, "and you *lied* to me!"

"Luna, no," Madame Hyde said. "You've got to understand—"

Luna leaned down and snatched *The Wisdom of Witchdom* off the floor. "This book is as big a fake as you are!" she said, flinging it into the fireplace.

"No!" Madame Hyde shouted, lunging for it—but the

book landed near the back of the fireplace. It curled, blackened, and burst into flame.

Madame Hyde stamped her foot, then whirled about. "All right!" she said. "I admit I use a little fakery here and there, a little harmless showmanship—but only to inspire people to *believe!* Luna, I swear, my powers are real!"

"I don't believe you," Luna said. "I think you're just what Max says you are—a fraud and a swindler. And that means there's no magickal spell for walking on air or time travel or anything. It means that Max and I are really stuck here in 1939, and we'll never get home. And it means that I walked off a third-floor landing and almost killed myself!" She choked back a sob, then put her face in her hands. "I've been such a fool!"

Madame Hyde reached out to the girl.

Luna pulled away. "No!" she snapped. "Don't touch me!"

In the corner, the clock chimed eleven.

Time Trooper 7 stopped the hovercar. "We'll pursue them on foot," it said. The doors opened and the boarding ramps were lowered. The robots hurried out of the vehicle. Trooper 7 stepped off the ramp and turned to Grady. "Stay in the vehicle!" it said.

"I don't take orders from machines!" Grady replied— and he leaped straight at Trooper 7, putting his shoulder into its metal chest plate. Trooper 7 staggered backward and clattered onto the pavement.

Grady jumped up and took off running. His shoulder throbbed from the impact with the robot. *Remind me never to do THAT again!*

Behind Grady, Trooper 7 rocked on its back like an overturned turtle. "Trooper 11! Help me up!" it shouted.

Trooper 11 came around the hovercar and pulled Trooper 7 to its feet.

"You capture the red-haired girl," Trooper 7 said. "I will capture the escaped prisoner."

"And the pink-skinned boy?" Trooper 11 asked.

"We'll deal with him later," Trooper 7 said. "Now, go!"

Just a few yards away, Grady Stubblefield crouched behind a beat-up orange Volkswagen. He heard metal footsteps clanking his way.

Grady got down on his hands and knees and peered under the car. He saw the shiny black metal boots of Trooper 7 walking by. A prickly sensation crept along his neck.

The boots stopped.

Grady froze, not daring to breathe. He felt something sticky. He looked and saw wet paint glistening on his arm. *Nice going, Stubblefield*, he told himself. *Great hiding place! Right behind Timebender!*

It was quiet for thirty or forty seconds—no sound of Trooper footsteps. Time crawled by like an inchworm, each second an eternity. The suspense was unbearable.

Finally, Grady bent down for another look under the car—

The black metal boots were gone.

Where did that Trooper go? he wondered.

He sat up—

And his spine bumped against something hard—the metal leg of a robot. Fingers of cold steel gripped his shoulder. Grady jerked his head around—

And stared into the metal face of Time Trooper 7.

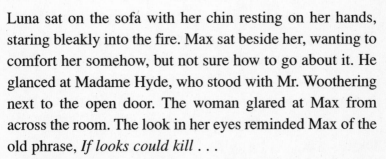

Luna sat on the sofa with her chin resting on her hands, staring bleakly into the fire. Max sat beside her, wanting to comfort her somehow, but not sure how to go about it. He glanced at Madame Hyde, who stood with Mr. Woothering next to the open door. The woman glared at Max from across the room. The look in her eyes reminded Max of the old phrase, *If looks could kill . . .*

Madame Hyde grabbed the white-haired man by the arm and yanked him roughly out the door.

Once they were outside the parlor, she said in a low voice, "Woothering, I want you to fetch my broom and bell of silver. Bring them to the pentacle in the atrium. Then I want you to prepare the Draconis Argentum."

"Madame!" the old man said, a wild and frightened look in his watery eyes. "The Draconis Argentum! That thing scares even me! Why do you want to convince this girl? Why not just let her go back to wherever she came from?"

"Do you *know* where she came from?" Madame Hyde asked.

Mr. Woothering shrugged. "I suppose they came from—"

"The future, Woothering!" Madame Hyde said. "Do you understand? They've come here from the twenty-first century!"

Mr. Woothering's eyes widened. "It must be some sort of hoax!"

"It's no hoax," Madame Hyde said. "I've seen the proof. Those two young people have knowledge of the future that I could use to gain power and wealth beyond imagining. The boy opposes me, but the girl, Luna—if I can win back her trust, I can make her my disciple. In time, she will tell me everything I need to know about the future."

"But how is that possible?" the old man asked. "Time travel is just a fantasy. How can you believe such a wild tale—"

"Say no more!" the woman snapped. Then she lowered her voice.

"Do as you're told! Prepare the Draconis Argentum!"

"Yes, Madame," Mr. Woothering said. He hurried away to carry out the woman's orders.

Madame Hyde returned to the crystal parlor and walked over to the red velvet sofa where Max and Luna sat together. "Luna, my dear," she said softly. "I know what you must think of me. You think I'm a fraud. You think I've lied to you—even made a fool of you."

Luna stared into the fire for a few moments. Then she looked up. "You fooled me once," she said stiffly. "You won't fool me again."

"Come with me," the woman said.

"No," the girl said. "I won't go anywhere with you—ever again."

"Luna, dear," Madame Hyde said softly, almost pleadingly. "Give me one last chance to prove myself to you. Please."

"She's not listening to you anymore," Max said.

There was a long silence in the room, broken only by the patient ticking of the clock in the corner.

"All right," Luna said. "One last chance." She rose unsteadily to her feet and walked toward Madame Hyde.

Max's jaw dropped open in shock. "Luna!" he said, jumping to his feet. "What are you doing?"

Madame Hyde put her arm around Luna, then looked over her shoulder at Max. The witch's eyes gleamed with triumph.

9

THE FALL OF THE DRAGON

Time Trooper 7 held Grady in a steel grip. "Do not attempt to escape," said the robot.

God, Grady prayed, *what do I do now?* Then a thought occurred to him: *Tell the truth.* Grady looked the Trooper in its metal faceplate. "I'm going to escape," he said.

"I forbid you to escape," said the robot.

"I'm going to escape anyway," Grady said.

The robot lifted Grady by the back of his shirt, so that the boy's feet were a foot off the ground. "No, you won't," said the robot.

"Yes, I will." Grady raised his arms straight up—and he slipped out of his shirt!

Trooper 7 stood with Grady's empty shirt in its hand. "What—?" it said.

"I'll take that!" Grady said, snatching his shirt. Then he dived between the robot's legs.

Trooper 7 bent over and tried to grab Grady—but the robot only succeeded in losing its balance and toppling onto its metal head.

Grady took off across the parking lot and headed for a tree-lined walk that led toward the middle of the campus. As he leaped over a hedge, he thought, *Robots are so stupid!*

Madame Hyde led Max and Luna into the atrium. The moonlight shone through the skylight, gray and sickly, making the floor look like skin infected with leprosy. The three of them waited in suspenseful silence for several minutes.

Max noticed that while most of the atrium floor tiles were made of dark-veined gray marble, there was an outline in the floor made from white marble. The outline shone faintly in the moonlight—a pentacle.

Finally, Mr. Woothering arrived, carrying a broom and a silver bell. Madame Hyde took the broom in her hands.

Max grinned at Madame Hyde. "A witch's broom?" he said. "What's next, a black cat and a boiling cauldron?"

"I'll soon wipe that grin off your silly face, young man," Madame Hyde said. "Midnight approaches—the witching hour."

The woman took the broom—a rough wooden pole with a bundle of twigs tied to the end. She danced around the pentacle, sweeping the broom through the air, chanting, "Staff of ash, protect me! / Twigs of birch, purify me. / Binding of willow, bind the forces of earth and sky to my will!"

Max rolled his eyes.

Next, Madame Hyde took the silver bell and rang it three times, saying in a loud voice, "With the ringing of this bell, / I begin this magick spell! / Let these silver vibrations / Ring forth my incantations!"

"Luna!" Max said. "You're not falling for her act all over again, are you?"

"I—I'm not sure what to think," Luna whispered, biting her lip.

Max turned away in frustration—and that's when he noticed that Mr. Woothering was gone, almost as if he had disappeared. *Interesting*, Max thought. *Mr. Woothering is always mysteriously absent whenever Madame Hyde demonstrates her "magickal powers."*

Allie dashed across the campus plaza, zigzagging around slower-moving college students on their way to class. Ahead was a two-story building with a sign over the front doors that read STUDENT UNION. She took a quick glance over her shoulder and saw a Time Trooper coming around the corner of a building. People screamed and ran to get out of the robot's way.

"Yikes!" Allie gasped.

She dashed up the steps and into the Student Union Building. Inside, she found herself in a lobby.

Along the wall were tables with signs that read:

Join the
Student
Democrats

SUPPORT
Hubert H.
Humphrey!

The Young
Republicans
Club

Nixon's
THE
One!

Behind the tables, two students argued about politics. One was a hippie girl with a big HUMPHREY FOR PRESIDENT button on her blue-and-purple granny dress, a circlet of flowers in her straight brown hair, leather sandals on her feet, and square-lensed granny glasses.

The other student had an equally large button that read VOTE REPUBLICAN. He wore a white shirt, narrow blue tie, black slacks, and a black sports coat. He had short crew-cut hair and wore black-rimmed glasses.

Allie interrupted. "Hide me, please! They're after me!"

"Who's after you?" the young Republican asked.

"Never mind," the hippie girl said. "Get under my table!"

Allie dived under a big HUMPHREY FOR PRESIDENT banner that hung across the front of the hippie girl's table.

Crash!

The glass door of the Student Union shattered into hundreds of fragments. Students screamed and scattered for the exits. A black-and-white robot lumbered through the opening. It was Trooper 11.

Trooper 11 clanked up to the table. "I apologize for the damage to your building," said the robot. "Where I come from, all doors open automatically. Have you citizens seen a female human with red hair and orthodontic appliances on her teeth?"

Knees trembling, the young Republican stared at Trooper 11. "W-what did she do?" he stammered.

"She has violated the Temporal Security Act," said the Trooper.

"Oh!" said the hippie girl, her voice shaking with fear. "Well, she ran up those stairs and out the back way! If you hurry, you can catch her!"

"Thank you for your cooperation, citizen," said Trooper 11. The robot turned and clanked up the stairs.

"You can come out now," the hippie girl said. "Mr. Iron-Pants is gone."

Allie came out from under the table.

"Thanks for not giving me away!" she said—then she dashed through the hole where the door used to be.

Mr. Woothering moved swiftly through the shadows and climbed a flight of stairs to a secret room on the third floor. Everything had to be ready when Madame Hyde spoke the words of the spell.

Alexander Mordin Woothering had faithfully served Madame Hyde for ten years. Before that, he had enjoyed a long career as a stage magician, Xander the Great. He could produce doves from his sleeves, make people appear out of thin air, saw people in half, and put them back together again. He never used sorcery, just illusion and trickery.

After his retirement, Madame Hyde employed him to design illusions to persuade her clients that she had "mystical powers." She paid him well, and he had installed all sorts of illusions in her mansion, such as self-lighting candles, hidden gas nozzles for explosions of flame, and a wire-suspended "air-walking" harness.

But Mr. Woothering's most complex illusion was a machine called the "Draconis Argentum," named after the mythical Silver Dragon. It was a huge mechanical dragon that Madame Hyde used to demonstrate her "power" to command the "forces of darkness." Unfortunately, the mechanical dragon didn't always work correctly. As Mr. Woothering sat down in the secret room, awaiting his cue to operate its wires, pulleys, and levers, he hoped the mechanical beast would behave itself tonight.

⊚ ⊚ ⊚

Toby crossed the street and sprinted down the sidewalk. Once he was safely away from the university, he quickly checked over his shoulder—*Excellent! No robots! They're probably chasing O'Dell and Stubblefield.*

Not watching where he was going, Toby sideswiped a lady pushing a baby stroller. "Watch it, lady!" he shouted.

Reaching a street corner, he paused for one more look toward the university campus. Still no sign of the Time Troopers. He checked the sign over the corner store: GRIMBLE'S DRUGSTORE. *Perfect!*

Toby stepped into the drugstore—then he stopped and stared.

There, directly in front of him, was a revolving rack of comic books—dozens and dozens of comic books. Toby's eyes lit up. They were brand-new, mint-condition, 1968 editions of *The Amazing Spiderman*, *The Incredible Hulk*, *The Fantastic Four*, *Captain America,* and so many more.

Toby stared at the prices printed on the covers. *Dude! These comics only cost twelve cents each!* He reached into his pocket and pulled out a wad of money—a five, three ones, five quarters, two dimes, and three pennies. Total: $9.48. He did the math: It would buy exactly seventy-nine comics. Total profit: *thousands!*

"Excellent!" he said aloud.

He stuffed the money back into his pocket and loaded

his arms with comics. Then he carried the comics over to the counter and stacked them in front of the clerk.

"You don't need to count them," Toby said. "There are seventy-nine."

The clerk, a bald man with a double chin and glasses, counted them anyway. When he was done, he said, "I count eighty-two." He pulled three *Silver Surfer* comics off the stack and set them aside. "*Now* there are seventy-nine."

Toby shrugged. "So I made a mistake."

"So you did," the clerk said, unsmiling. "That'll be nine dollars and forty-eight cents."

Toby shoved his cash across the counter. "It's all there."

"Sure it is," the clerk said as he began counting.

Toby began stuffing his backpack with comic books.

The clerk frowned. "Hey, kid!" he said. "What's with this Monopoly money?"

"Huh?" Toby said. "What's your problem?"

The clerk slammed the money on the counter. "These bills are dated 1999 . . . 1997 . . . 2001. . . . You do know this is 1968, don't you? Hand over those comic books, kid, and take your funny money someplace else!"

"Dude!" Toby said. "I paid for these and I'm taking them!"

"No you don't!" the clerk said. He dashed around the counter and grabbed Toby by the collar. With his free hand, he reached for the phone. "You're staying right here till the cops arrive!"

Max and Luna stood side by side in the middle of the atrium. Just a few steps away, in the center of the pentacle, Madame Hyde stood with her arms lifted high and her face tilted toward the skylight. Deathly gray moonlight shone in the woman's eyes and cast dark shadows in the hollows of her cheeks.

From the parlor came a mournful sound: the tolling of clock chimes. Midnight, the witching hour, had come.

Madame Hyde chanted, "Dragon, by thy fire and light, / I summon thee and conjure thee! / Come in all thy power and might! / As I will, so may it be!"

Even before she had finished chanting her spell, tendrils of smoke rose up out of the gloom at the far end of the atrium. The tendrils became billows. Gray clouds crawled like living, squirming masses across the floor, inching toward the place where Max and Luna stood.

In seconds, the fragrance of burning incense assaulted Max's nostrils. The fragrance was half-sweet, half-bitter, half-pleasant, half-pungent. It smelled of sandalwood and pine, juniper and thistle, allspice and cloves. The smoke aggravated Max's breathing. He pulled out his asthma inhaler and took a puff. It didn't help.

Billows of pale blue smoke rolled across the pentacle, surrounding Madame Hyde as she continued to chant louder and louder. Coils of incense-laden fumes swirled in the air. Max blinked his burning eyes.

He turned to Luna to say something—but when he saw the girl's face, he forgot what he had planned to say. Luna's eyes were alight with awe and fascination. Madame Hyde's chanting was drawing Luna's soul back into the realm of Darkness.

The smoke was turning to smog—a blue haze that smudged the air of the atrium from floor to ceiling. Max struggled for breath—and not just because of the burning incense. It was *fear* that tightened his lungs—a dark dread of an unknown threat that lurked somewhere within the smoke and gloom.

Whooosh! Out of the smoke came a burst of flame!

A huge, snakelike shadow loomed out of the darkness and smoke at the far end of the atrium. Two eyes, like red embers, peered through the billowing plumes of smoke. The snaking thing towered nearly to the top of the atrium. It swayed back and forth—then it lunged forward, into the rectangle of leprous gray moonglow that shone down from the skylight. The creature's skin reflected the moonlight in silvery glints and sparkles.

Madame Hyde continued chanting within the circle of the pentacle as clouds of smoke coiled around her.

Max was instantly overshadowed by a sense of horror— a *familiar* horror. This thing that reared up before him was eerily similar to the Dragon he had met in a long-ago time, in a place called Eden. The memory sent an electric tingle of fear down his spine.

Could it be true? Was the Silver Dragon here? Had Madame Hyde somehow managed to invoke a personal appearance by that ancient Enemy? Max wondered.

"Max!" Luna said, her voice a frightened mouse-squeak. "What's *that?*" She pointed up at the swaying dragon-thing. Before Max could answer—

Whooosh! Another ball of flame blasted from the gaping mouth of the dragon-thing. Luna jumped.

At that moment, Max's fear vanished. In a flash, he *knew* that something was not right with this swaying monster. Despite the shadows that wrapped the atrium and the haze of incense that stung his eyes, Max could somehow tell that this was not what he had first thought it to be. It might be dragon-shaped—but it definitely wasn't the Dragon of Eden, the Enemy who had tempted Max and his friends on their first journey through time. There was something unnatural, almost mechanical, about the movements of *this* dragon.

Whooosh! Another blast of flame—and this time, it was accompanied by a grinding, clattering, groaning sound. The silvery dragon-shape swayed and tottered drunkenly in the moonlight.

Luna screamed and clutched at Max.

Max glanced at Madame Hyde—and saw that the woman had stopped chanting. She seemed to be as alarmed and afraid as Luna. Clearly, the dragon-thing was behaving in a way that Madame Hyde didn't expect.

Clutching at Luna's arm, Max said, "Get back, Luna! Get back!"

As the dragon-thing tumbled toward the marble floor, Max and Luna scrambled to get out of its way. So did Madame Hyde—but she wasn't fast enough.

◎ ◎ ◎

After leaving the Student Union, Allie doubled back to the street where she had last seen Toby. Reaching the edge of the campus, Allie heard it: horns honking. People shouting. A man yelling, "Come back here, you little punk!" Another voice shouting, "Dude! Out of my way!"

Allie's heart leaped. "Toby!" Dashing in the direction of the noise, she came upon a traffic jam. Cars screeched to a halt and drivers pounded their horns as a boy in a dirty white tee shirt and grass-stained cargo pants chugged across the street. Under a sign that read GRIMBLE'S DRUGSTORE, a bald man shook his fist and swore, "If I ever catch you in my store again—"

"Toby!" Allie called.

Toby's head snapped around in surprise. He came running across the grass. "Dude!" he said. "Let's get out of here!"

"Sure," Allie said. "Let's go that way, over by the dorms. But not so fast—let's just jog."

Toby glanced over his shoulder. No one was chasing him. "I've got a better idea," he said. "Let's walk."

So they walked.

"What were you doing in that drugstore?" Allie asked. "And why was that guy yelling at you?"

"Who knows?" Toby said. "I just wanted to buy some comic books."

"Comic books!" Allie said. "We don't have time for comic books! Don't you know how much trouble we're in?"

"I know, I know! Don't remind me!"

"Where's your backpack?"

"I left it in the drugstore."

"Want to go back for it?"

"Dude! Are you crazy?"

Max and Luna peered through the smoky gloom as the echoes from the dragon's fall died away. Luna looked at Max. "Where's Madame Hyde?" she asked.

"She must have been—," Max began, then stopped.

A muffled moan came from somewhere beneath the crumpled, shattered mound of the dragon-machine.

"She's alive!" Max said in amazement. "She's underneath that thing!" Max ran forward, toward the sound of the woman's moans. Luna stayed where she was, eyes wide and staring, biting her knuckles.

As Max neared the fallen dragon, he noticed it looked

more like a cartoon version of the Silver Dragon—a silly, goofy-looking, fake dragon that wouldn't have fooled anyone—if not for the darkness and smoke.

Max reached the side of the dragon-thing. Coughing, wheezing, eyes burning, Max could just make out the shapeless, fallen mass that snaked across the floor, disappearing into the smoke and gloom at the far end of the atrium. He heard the moans again, but he couldn't be sure exactly where they came from.

Then the lights came on.

Max winced. The light poured through the gray, smoky haze from recessed fixtures in the atrium ceiling. Even through the smog of incense, the light seemed blindingly bright. Eyes watering, Max got his first good look at the dragon-thing. It was made of cloth with a coating of metallic paint. The silvery cloth covered a riblike structure, and many of those wooden ribs were now broken, splintered, and sticking up through rips in the silvery fabric.

"Oh, no!" said a man's voice. "I've killed her!"

Max looked to his left and saw Mr. Woothering running across the floor, his eyes wide and his white hair affright. The old man's hard-soled shoes clattered on the marble floor as he ran.

There was a muffled sound of tearing fabric. "Woothering!" came a woman's voice from inside the gullet of the collapsed dragon. Then Max saw moving ripples in the cloth of the dragon's neck. Madame Hyde had apparently ripped her way through the underside of the thing and was now crawling out toward the head.

Max went around to the front of the dragon's goofy-looking face and pried the mouth open with both hands. The construction of the thing was surprisingly lightweight, and seemed to consist of pinewood and thin metal control rods—all of it now broken and ruined. The nose of the thing seemed to be made of a light metal, probably tin, and had a little nozzle poking out of it—no doubt the gas jet that created the ball-of-fire effect.

Max held the dragon mouth open as Mr. Woothering reached in and took Madame Hyde's hand, helping her climb out of the dragon contraption.

"Oh!" the woman shrieked as she clambered to her feet. "Oh!"

Her raven-black hair was a mad tangle that hung in her eyes. The skin on her arms bore several bleeding scratches. Her simple white gown was smudged with grime and had a big rip down around the hem. She was a mess.

"Madame Hyde!"

The startled woman turned at the sound of Luna's voice. She pushed the stray strands of hair from in front of her wide blue eyes. She didn't look much like a powerful, self-confident witch anymore. In fact, in her rumpled condition, she didn't look like she could command a mop and bucket, much less the forces of magick.

Luna stared coldly at the woman she had once idolized.

"'Give me one last chance to prove myself,' you said. Well, you've had your chance, Madame Hyde. And you've proved to me—" She choked, and her eyes puddled with tears. "You've proved exactly what you are."

A black strand of hair drooped in front of Madame Hyde's face. She blew it aside and looked like she was ready to cry.

"M-Madame," Mr. Woothering stammered. "I—I don't know what went wrong. I—"

"Oh, shut up!" Madame Hyde shrieked. She knotted one delicate white fist and swung it at Mr. Woothering. He backed away from the blow. Madame Hyde windmilled around and ended up smack on her bottom. "Ooooh!" she moaned, hanging her head.

Max extended his hand to help Madame Hyde up—

But suddenly he couldn't see her. The bright ceiling lights had gone out, and the atrium was plunged into darkness. Max knew it beyond a shadow of a doubt—

Something terrible was about to happen.

10

THE MARK OF EVIL

A rock beat drifted down from a second-story window of the dormitory. Someone was playing an album by the Doors.

On the sidewalk below the window, Allie and Toby hurried along. They continually checked behind them and around them as they walked.

"If we can work our way back to the parking lot," Allie said, "without running into any Time Troopers—"

"Got you!" said a voice behind them.

"Aaaagh!" Toby yelled.

Allie whirled and saw something spring out at her from the bushes. She screamed—

"Grady, you brat!" Allie said.

Grady laughed. "Allie! Toby! I thought I'd never see you guys again!"

"Dude!" Toby whined. "You gave me a heart attack!"

"That was a horrible trick," Allie said—then she hugged him. "But I've never been more glad to see anyone in my life! At least we're all together. How did you get away from the Time Troopers?"

"I'll tell you all about it later," Grady said. "Right now, we've got to get back to the car and timebend out of here!"

The lights had gone out in the atrium. Somewhere in the darkness, Luna gave a startled cry. In seconds, Max's eyes began to adjust, and he could see that the atrium was not totally dark. Pale moonlight still streamed down through the skylight.

Seconds passed, each second an agony of suspense and terror of the unknown.

Then came a *crash*—a grinding, splintering, shattering sound of glass breaking.

Something had fallen through the top of the building, crashing through the skylight. It fell through the air of the atrium with a pounding of leathery wings, as loud as the thunder of helicopter blades. There was a sound like the scrabble of metallic claws on marble tile, the slap of scaly leather on cold stone.

Then a great mass reared up before them, lit from above by silvery moonlight, with inky shadows underneath. The thing gave the impression of great, spreading wings, shaped like bat wings but as broad as the wings of a Cessna airplane. Its body was huge and dinosaur-like, and it stood on four legs. Its head swayed on a long, snaking neck. Its skin was covered in thousands of mirrorlike scales and encrusted with gleaming gemstones. The eyes of the beast blazed with red fire, and the pupils of its eyes were vertical slits of infinite darkness. Smoke puffed from its nostrils, and its forked tongue flicked out between silvery fangs.

The *real* Silver Dragon had arrived.

@ @ @

Allie, Grady, and Toby nervously made their way across the middle of the campus. Toby gave them a fright when he thought he spotted a Time Trooper in front of the Warren G. Harding School of Political Science—but it turned out to be nothing but a statue.

"We'll make it back to Timebender," Allie said as she walked between Grady and Toby. "We *have* to make it back to Timebender, and the Time Troopers *have* to come chasing after us—or we wouldn't have seen ourselves in Max's backyard."

Grady nodded in agreement.

"The only question is—" She shuddered. "What happens after we *leave* Max's backyard? Will the Time Troopers catch us—or will we get away?"

Toby squealed, pointing ahead. "There they are!"

Allie and Grady looked up ahead. The two Time Troopers were crossing the campus green. Students stopped in their tracks, screamed, and ran, clearing a path for the two robots. The Troopers' metal heads swiveled back and forth, scanning for the time fugitives.

"Over here!" Grady said. They hid behind a big hedge in front of the Language Arts Building.

Allie peeked through a hole in the hedge. "Oh, no!" she said. "They're coming this way!"

◎ ◎ ◎

It was a moment Max had hoped would never come again, a moment he had foreseen only in his worst nightmares: He was face-to-face with the Silver Dragon once more. He quickly whispered a prayer for courage and wisdom, then—

"Impressive entrance," Max said. "Of course, most people just ring the doorbell." He glanced at Madame Hyde and Mr. Woothering. The woman had somehow gotten to her feet. The two of them now stood rooted to the floor, paralyzed with shock and fear.

Flames licked the Dragon's lips. "Well, well," the beast said. "Max McCrane! We meet again." A threatening rumble came from his throat and a puff of gray smoke blew from his flaring nostrils.

"Max!" a voice called from the darkness behind him. Max turned and saw Luna stepping forward from the gloom, her eyes staring, her platinum-gold hair gleaming in the moonglow. "This is the Dragon you were talking about! The *real* Dragon that you met in the Garden of Eden!"

"Yes, I am he," the Dragon said, with a polite bow of his head. His lips twisted in a charming, reptilian smile. "And you, my dear—you are Luna Skyes."

"You know my name!" Luna said, delighted.

"I was made aware of you," the Dragon said, "soon after you came here from the future."

"O Dragon!" Madame Hyde called out. "I never imagined I could actually summon—"

The Dragon whirled on Madame Hyde. "You miserable bungler!"

"I—," Madame Hyde stammered. "I— I— I—"

"First, you tried to call me with that ridiculous spell," the Dragon said. "And then what did you do? You had this fool here—" The beast pointed a silvery claw at Mr. Woothering. "You had him impersonate me with this absurd mechanical contraption! Of all the witches and wizards in my dark domain, you are surely the most incompetent, boneheaded blunderer of all!"

"I— I— I—," the woman stammered again.

"Out of my sight—both of you!" the Dragon roared.

Madame Hyde and Mr. Woothering trembled and shrank from the Dragon's sulphurous breath, but their feet refused to move.

Whoooooosh! A billow of flame roared from the gorge of the Silver Dragon.

Madame Hyde shrieked! Mr. Woothering wailed! The two frauds turned and ran into each other, knocking each other flat. Then they clawed at each other and scrambled over each other, each trying to be the first to the door. Their panic-driven footsteps echoed across the atrium. In seconds Madame Hyde had reached the front door, with Mr. Woothering only a step and a half behind her. The woman flung the door open, and then both of them were gone from sight. The *clack-clack-clack* of their footsteps faded away.

"That woman," the Dragon said, "has been a wretched disappointment from the start. She and Woothering were just small-time con artists." The Dragon turned to Luna. "But you, my dear," he said with a bewitching smile. "I can see that you are a human creature of great intelligence. You and I could become mighty allies. With the wealth and power I could give you—"

"Luna," Max said, "don't listen to this liar!"

"Be quiet, Max!" Luna said.

Max looked dumbfounded. "But I thought you had given up on witchcraft!"

"You thought wrong, Max," Luna said. "Sure, I was disillusioned when Madame Hyde turned out to be a fake—but now I've met the Dragon! He's offering me wealth and power—everything I've ever dreamed of!"

"Yes, Luna!" the Dragon said. "Whatever you want

shall be yours! Money! Fame! Power! Secret knowledge! All this and more will be yours!"

"Luna," Max said. "People weren't meant to have that kind of power. God says—"

"Max's God," the Dragon says, "only wants to keep you powerless and make you feel guilty for doing what you want to do. Let *me* be your god, Luna, and I will impose no laws or restrictions on you. You have no need of God. Join me, Luna! Receive my mark, and we will be together until the end of time."

"Together in Darkness, Luna," Max said. "Together in the Pit."

"Quiet, Max!" Luna shouted, mesmerized by the Dragon. "I *want* the Dragon's power! I *want* the Dragon's mark!"

"No, Luna!" Max said. "You don't know what you're doing!"

"I know exactly what I'm doing, Max," Luna said fiercely. "The Dragon will give me everything I want—not just power, but a place to belong!" Tears welled in Luna's eyes and trembled there, refusing to fall.

"Luna," he said, "you already have a place to belong. Your family—"

"What do you know about my family, Max?" she said. "All my dad cares about is his art shows and taking his paintings all around the country. I hardly even know my dad. And all my mom cares about is my straight-A sister, Little Miss Brains! And who am I? I'm nobody. I'm the one who's always in the way. I'm the one who gets told, 'Why don't you get good grades like your sister?' No one listens to me, Max. No one cares if I live or die—except the Dragon."

"I didn't know you felt that way," Max said.

"Now can you see why I want this power? In my ordinary so-called 'life,' I'm powerless, I'm a *nobody*. But when I receive the Dragon's mark, I'll have everything I want—and I'll be *somebody*."

"What about the cost, Luna?" asked Max. "Your eternal soul! Think about that!"

"I don't believe in eternity," Luna said. "I believe in *now*. I've made my choice."

Luna took a step toward the evil beast, but Max leaped in front of her.

"Out of my way, Max!" Luna said.

"Yes, Max McCrane," the Dragon rumbled. "She has made her choice!"

"Wait, Luna!" Max said, ignoring the Dragon. "Hear me out! I know you don't want to do evil. I know you think that you can use this power to do good."

"Of course," Luna said. "I only want to do white magick. I would never use the Dragon's power to hurt anyone."

"You don't know how deceptive the Dragon is," Max said. "He'll give you this power, and he'll let you do some good things with it—at first. But this power comes from an evil source, Luna! You can't use evil to do good! You think you can control it, but eventually it will control you! And then it will be too late to back out."

"Get out of my way, Max," Luna said. She pushed past him and approached the Dragon. "I'm ready," she said.

Max prayed silently, *Isn't there anything I can do, God? Anything at all?*

Luna stood before the Dragon, her face tilted toward the moonglow. The Dragon towered over her and raised one shining silver foreclaw.

"Listen to me, Luna," Max said. "It's not too late! You can still call upon God right now!"

But Luna didn't seem to hear a word Max said.

"Luna Skyes, daughter of Earth," the Dragon said, "do you offer yourself freely to my service in exchange for the power I have promised you?"

"I do," Luna said firmly. "As I will, so may it be."

"Then receive my mark upon your soul, Luna Skyes," said the Dragon. "As you will, so may it ever be."

And the Dragon reached out toward Luna's brow.

"Luna!" Max shouted. "Don't do this! Don't—"

A brilliant spark of light, like an electric arc, leaped from the foreclaw of the Dragon to the face of Luna Skyes. The girl screamed—

The echo of her cry rang throughout the atrium.

Luna swayed, then toppled backward. Max ran forward and caught her in his arms. The girl's eyes rolled toward the back of her head, and her mouth fell slack. Max eased her gently to the cold marble floor. An angry red mark glowed like a hot coal upon her forehead. In seconds, the mark faded from her brow—but Max knew it was still burned into her soul.

"Oh, no," he groaned. "Oh, no."

Allie, Grady, and Toby crouched behind the hedge.

"Allie," Grady said, "do you think the Troopers saw us?"

"I don't know!" she said. "What should we do?"

Grady thought quickly. "Okay, listen," he said. "If they come after us, we scatter in three directions."

"Good idea." Allie nodded. "The two of them can't catch all three of us!"

"Right," Grady said. "If we get separated, we all take different routes to the parking lot. We'll meet at Timebender—got it?"

"Dude!" Toby said, trembling. "Why did I ever let you guys drag me along on this trip?"

"Answer me, Toby!" Grady said. "Do you understand the plan?"

"Yeah," Toby said. "Dude! I'm not stupid."

Allie peeked through the hole in the hedge. "Hey!" she said. "I don't see them anywhere. The Time Troopers— they're just gone!"

"Well, what do you know?" Grady said. "Looks like we got a break! Come on guys! To the parking lot!"

Allie, Grady, and Toby left their hiding place and dashed out into the open.

The two Time Troopers crouched on the roof of the Cafeteria Building, watching as Grady, Allie, and Toby dashed by on their way to the parking lot.

Trooper 7 said, "You were right, Trooper 11. This is the perfect place from which to spot them. The time fugitives will lead us straight to their time machine."

Trooper 11 nodded. "They have walked into our trap."

11

POWER TRAP

Grady, Allie, and Toby crept up behind some bushes at one end of the parking lot. "I'm hungry," Toby said. "Either of you dorks got any candy bars?"

Allie reached into her purse and pulled out a tin of Altoids. "Here," she said. "Have some mints and be quiet."

"I don't want mints," Toby said. "I want chocolate." But he popped three mints into his mouth anyway.

Grady and Allie raised their heads and looked around the lot. "There's the hovercar," Grady said, nodding toward the far end of the lot. "It's empty."

"I don't see the Time Troopers anywhere," Allie said.

"Me, neither," Grady said. He thought quickly, forming a plan. "If the Time Troopers are waiting for us," he said, "we won't have much time. Whoever gets into Timebender first has to turn on the power, punch in some coordinates, and be ready to hit ENTER, got it?"

"Got it," Allie said.

"Yeah, I got it," Toby said, clutching the tin of mints.

"Are we ready?" Allie asked.

"As ready as we'll ever be," Grady said. "Let's go."

The three time fugitives jumped up and sprinted across the parking lot. Grady's eyes scanned in every direction as they ran. Still no Time Troopers. So far, so good—

Allie screamed!

Grady looked. Time Trooper 7 jumped up from behind a 1966 Ford Fairlane and stepped right into their path. "Halt!" it said, putting out one hand. The three humans skidded to a stop.

"Split up!" said Grady.

The three time travelers took off in three different directions—Grady to the left, Allie to the right, and Toby dashing back the way he came. Trooper 7 hesitated for a split second, then went after Toby.

Allie saw Timebender parked up ahead, just twenty yards away. In seconds she would be there—

Then she saw something out of the corner of her eye: Trooper 11! The robot was crouched behind a red '58 Edsel about ten yards to Allie's left—and Grady was running straight toward it.

"Grady, look out!" Allie shouted—too late.

Time Trooper 11 leaped out from behind the Edsel.

Grady had no time to stop. He ran—*wham!*—into the robot. Trooper 11's arms flailed as it tried to regain its balance—then it tumbled over onto its back with Grady on top of its chest. Grady jumped up and sprinted toward Timebender.

"Halt!" Trooper 11 called, rocking helplessly on its back, unable to get up. "You are under arrest!"

Kneeling at Luna's side, Max looked up at the Dragon with cold fury in his eyes. "She doesn't understand what she's doing! She doesn't understand what eternity means!"

"She has chosen," the Dragon said. "That's all that matters. And what about you, Max McCrane?"

"Huh?" Max said. "What about me?"

"Why don't you join me, too?" the Dragon said, smiling craftily. "With my power flowing through you, there is no limit to what you could accomplish."

"You already made me that offer," Max said. "I turned it down thousands of years ago. I haven't changed my mind."

"You choose the losing side," the Dragon said smugly.

"I'm on the side of the Creator, and He can't lose."

"The Creator has already lost your friend Luna," the Dragon said. "Her soul has slipped through His fingers. He is always losing souls like hers. Down through history, millions of human souls have joined my cause. Do you know why, Max?"

"Because you're such a clever liar," Max said.

"No," the Dragon said, advancing toward Max. Tongues of flame licked the Dragon's lips. "Because evil is stronger than good. Hate is stronger than love. Destruction is stronger than creation. This Creator you serve, Elyon the Most High, has limited His own power—*but I have not*. He will not take human souls by force or deception—*but I will*. The Creator made a fatal mistake at the beginning of time. He chose to create beings with a will that was not *His* will, with the power to defy Him."

Luna moaned and rolled her head from side to side. Max looked down at her. The thought of what she had just done made him sick inside.

"The Creator could have made creatures," the Dragon continued, "that would never disobey Him, never grieve Him. He could have made creatures that would praise and adore Him throughout eternity, with never a thought of sin or rebellion—but no! He wanted creatures who were the essence of otherness and apartness. And we, the Dark Emissaries, exploit this whenever we can."

"You've seen Him face-to-face, yet you still can't understand Him," Max said. "Face it, Dragon, you're finished. Doomed. Why do you keep fighting Him?"

"To hurt Him!" the Dragon said, stamping his silver-clawed foot upon the marble floor. "Whenever I can drag a human soul into the Pit with me, I make Him suffer! For some unknowable reason, He loves you miserable, worthless creatures—so I use His love against Him. Whenever I can destroy what He loves, I have won a small victory. Perhaps an eternity in the Pit won't be so unbearable—if only I can hurt Him enough."

"Max," Luna moaned. She reached up and touched her forehead. "I feel—strange," she said. "It's true, isn't it! I am a *real* witch, with *real* power!"

"Yes, Luna," the Dragon said. "It's true."

Luna jumped to her feet and stared at her hands. "I can feel it! I can use this power any way I want to!"

"Yes," the Dragon said, smiling. "Any way you want to."

"Finally, I can *be* somebody!" Luna said, a gleam of triumph in her eyes. "From now on, people will look *up* to me! From now on, people had better stay out of *my* way!"

"Luna," Max said. "Listen to me! It's not too late! Please, give up this power!"

"Oh, Max," Luna said, turning her back on him. "You're really getting tiresome! Will you shut up and leave me—"

"Luna," Max said, "I care about you. Even after everything you've done, after the way you tricked me. I care about you! Maybe I'm stupid for caring more about your eternal soul than you do, but I can't help it, Luna! You've got to listen to me! I know that if you'll just call on God right now, He—"

"Grrr! I've had it with you, Max!" Luna said through clenched teeth. Then she whirled about, pointed her finger at Max, and said, "Just *drop dead*, will you?"

A blinding flash of light exploded from Luna's pointed finger. The flash crackled into Max's chest.

Max's mouth dropped open and his glasses flew off. He crumpled, a look of utter surprise on his face.

"Max!" Luna cried.

Max hit the floor with a sickening smack, and instantly curled up with his hands clutching his chest and his knees tucked up against his elbows. His eyes were shut tightly. He lay in a pool of moonlight on the atrium floor—

And he didn't move.

Allie flung open the driver's-side door and jumped in behind the wheel. She reached over to the glove box, flipped the power switch to ON, then grabbed the computer keyboard. She was punching random coordinates into the keypad when Grady got to the car, panting for breath.

"Where's Toby?" Allie called through the window.

Grady looked around. "There!" he said. "I see him! The other Trooper has him!"

Over by the edge of the parking lot, Trooper 7 was lifting Toby off the ground.

"Allie!" Grady said through the broken window. "I'm going to get Toby and bring him back. Wait twenty seconds, then hit ENTER!"

"But—," Allie began.

"Trust me!" Grady shouted.

Before Allie could protest, Grady was gone.

Max lay unmoving on the cold marble floor.

Luna threw herself down at Max's side. She slid one arm under his head and raised him slightly. "I killed him!" Luna said, looking up at the Dragon. "I killed him!"

The Dragon took a few steps back. "This wasn't supposed to happen," he said.

"I didn't know," Luna said. "I didn't know the power you gave me could hurt someone like this! I didn't know that I could just say—"

Luna was interrupted by a faint sound—the clink of metal on marble. She looked down at the floor. Something had fallen from Max's pocket. She reached down and picked it up, holding it in the palm of her hand: a cross of gold. The cross became blurry as Luna looked at it. She closed her fingers around the little gold cross, and a tear spilled from her eye and ran slowly down her cheek.

"Oooh!"

Startled by the sound from Max's lips, Luna looked down at his face. He was grimacing, as if in pain.

"Oooh!" he groaned again. "It hurts."

"Max!" Luna cried, cradling his head. "Max, you're alive!"

"Ow!" Max said, flinching. "Ow, that really hurts!"

"What hurts?" Luna said. "Where?"

"My—ow! My chest!" Max winced. "It hurts where you—Set me down!"

Luna let Max's head down gently onto the floor.

The face of the Dragon loomed out of the darkness, eyeing Max. Twin puffs of smoke blew from its nostrils.

"Oh, Max!" Luna said. "I—I'm so sorry I did this to you! I didn't mean it when I said—"

"I know, Luna," Max said through pain-clenched teeth.

One thousand eight, one thousand nine . . .

Allie counted to herself as she watched Grady through the broken rear window of the Volkswagen.

An electronic voice made her jump: "Step out of the vehicle!"

Allie screamed and turned around. There, just a few feet from the driver's-side door, stood Trooper 11. Somehow, the robot had gotten onto its feet. In its fist was a crystal-lensed pistol device—and it was aimed at Allie.

Heart fluttering with fear, Allie punched the lock button on the driver's door, and kept counting to herself: *One thousand ten, one thousand eleven . . .*

"It is useless to lock the door," Trooper 11 said. "Surrender now!"

◎ ◎ ◎

Luna looked skyward. Tears ran down her face. "God! Please!" she sobbed. In her hand, she gripped the little golden cross.

Somewhere in the darkness, the Dragon roared in rage.

"God! Help us!" Luna pleaded again. "Max is hurt, and it's all my fault! Everything's my fault! I've made such a mess of everything! God, I know I don't deserve any favors, but if You'll help Max right now, I'll do anything You ask! Please!"

"Your prayer has been heard, Laura Skyes."

A golden light shone in the darkness, surrounding Max and Luna in its soft glow.

A short distance away, the Dragon snorted and backed away from the light, seeking refuge in the shadows.

"Hello, Laura," said a rich, golden voice from the light.

Luna's voice shook. "Who's there?" she asked. "And why did you call me Laura?"

"Don't be afraid," said the voice from the light. "I have come to help." The light took shape—a shape that was humanlike but not human. It came closer and bent down to Max, covering him with its golden warmth. Max's face softened and relaxed, as if the pain had suddenly left him.

Luna looked up at the golden being. She tried to see the light-being's face, but the golden light made it impossible to make out any details. "You called me—"

"Laura is the name your parents gave you," the golden being said. "Laura Skyes. It's a lovely name. Why did you change it?"

"I made up the name Luna," she said, biting her lip. "I wanted a name that sounds mystical and magical—a name that would make me feel important."

"And now, what name would you choose?"

"Now? Now, I would like to be Laura again."

"Very well, then," the light-being said. "From this moment on, Laura is your name."

"Gavriyel!"

Laura looked down when she heard Max's voice. His eyes were open. He was smiling up at the golden light.

"Gavriyel," Max said again. "I was hoping you'd come. It's because Luna—It's because Laura prayed, isn't it?"

"Yes," Gavriyel said. "The One whose Name is above all names heard Laura's prayer and sent me to help you."

"I don't understand," Laura said, her voice breaking. "How could God hear my prayer when I don't belong to Him?"

"The moment you prayed that prayer," Gavriyel said, "you made a new beginning. You confessed your guilt, making no excuses. There was genuine sorrow and repentance in your voice. The golden cross in your hand symbolized your hope—even though it was a faint and slender hope—in the One who gave His life for you. Laura Skyes, you called upon the Name of God, and everyone who calls upon the Name of the Lord will be saved."

"Gavriyel!" a voice rumbled from the darkness. Max and Laura turned and saw the Dragon step out of the shadows and into the pale moonlight. "The Most High cannot cheat me of my prize! The girl bears my mark upon her! She is mine!"

Gavriyel looked at Laura. "I see no mark on her."

The Dragon looked at Laura in astonishment. "My mark! It's gone!"

"A girl named Luna was marked by you," Gavriyel said. "But this girl, Laura, is a new creature. Her soul has been marked and sealed by the one true God."

The Dragon flew into a rage. He reared his head back on his sinuous neck and roared, expelling a great billow of fire and smoke.

"Oh, hush up, evil one!" Gavriyel said. "No one wants you here, so by the Name that is above all names—begone!"

The effect of Gavriyel's command was astonishing. It was as if the voice of Gavriyel were a mighty wind. Instantly, the Silver Dragon dissolved into thousands of silver shreds that fluttered away on the wind, swirling off into some unseen dimension. Even as it disintegrated, the Dragon cursed and screamed and swore vengeance. But within seconds, there was nothing left of the Dragon but an echo. Then, even the echo was gone.

"Take Max's hand, Laura," the golden Emissary said. "Help him to his feet."

Laura stood, then helped Max up.

"I don't get it," Laura said. "It's too good to be true! Max is healed, I've been saved from the Dragon, and—oh, no!" She shut her eyes and groaned.

"What?" Max said.

"I just remember what a mess I made of things," Laura said. "We're still stuck in 1939, with no way to get home."

"Oh, yeah," Max said. "I forgot about that." He looked up at the Emissary. "Gavriyel—any ideas?"

Grady reached the place where Toby struggled in the grip of Trooper 7. "Toby!" Grady yelled. "Toss me the mints!"

Toby looked at his hand and saw the tin of Altoids. "Dude!" he yelled. "Are you crazy?"

"Do you want to get home?" Grady shouted. "Toss me those mints!"

Toby tossed the mints. Grady caught them on the run and dashed around behind Trooper 7. He jumped up onto the robot's back, wrapped his left arm around its neck, and pulled himself up. With his right hand, he brought the tin of Altoids around like a hammer, right into the lens of the robot's right visual receiver—*smash!* Then he hit the left visual receiver with the tin—*smash!*

"Help!" Trooper 7 said. "I'm damaged! I can't receive visual input!"

The robot dropped Toby, and the boy landed on his tail-bone. "Ooof! Ow!"

Grady let go of the robot's neck, landed lightly on his feet, scrambled around the robot, and yanked Toby off the asphalt. "Let's go!" he yelled.

Back at Timebender, Allie counted, *One thousand nineteen, one thousand twenty*—Allie's finger hovered over the ENTER key. She looked out the window—

And saw Grady and Toby running toward the car!

She pressed ENTER, then leaned over and opened the passenger-side door.

"Oh, hurry, hurry, hurry!" she said, wringing her hands.

"You leave me no choice," Trooper 11 said, grabbing the door handle.

Grady reached the car just ahead of Toby. He shoved Toby into the backseat, then jumped into the front.

There was an ear-splitting screech of tortured metal as Trooper 11 pulled the driver's-side door off the hinges. Allie screamed—and so did Toby.

"Now," the robot said, "step out of the—"

Time Trooper 11 stopped in midsentence, holding the car door in one hand.

Timebender was gone—again.

12

THE INVASION

Trooper 7 wandered blindly, bumping into parked cars. "Trooper 11! Trooper 11! Where are you?"

"I'm right here," Trooper 11 said.

"Give me your hand!" Trooper 7 said. "Lead me back to the hovercar. There are some spare visual receptors in the emergency kit."

Trooper 11 took Trooper 7's hand and led the blind robot back to the hovercar.

"They're leaving a fresh trail of time particles," Trooper 11 said. "If we hurry, we can still catch them!"

Grady, Allie, and Toby looked out the windows of the Volkswagen. Gripping the steering wheel, Allie took a deep, frightened breath. "Guys . . . ?" she said.

"Oh, no!" Grady said, staring.

"Dude!" Toby said, his mouth hanging open.

They were surrounded on all sides by an alien-looking landscape. The sky was yellow. Strange red clouds boiled in the upper atmosphere. The ground looked like a gray slag that had cooled to a hard, rippled stone. All around were high, volcanic mountains, spewing lava and greasy smoke.

Allie took a breath—then wrinkled her nose. "Eeww!" she said. "It smells like rotten eggs!"

"Get us out of here," Toby said.

"Wait," Grady said. "If we're not careful, our next time jump might take us to a time when there is no Earth at all—and then where will we be?"

Allie thought a moment, then opened her purse and took out Max's spiral-bound notebook. "You know," she said, "the answer's got to be somewhere in this notebook." She opened it and began flipping pages—then stopped at a page she had not noticed before:

TIMEBENDER CODES

Auto-Return Code: ESCAPE
(Returns Timebender to the point of last departure)

Homing Code: ALT + TAB
(Returns Timebender to time and place of last memory reset)

"That's it!" Allie said. "That's what we need!"

Grady leaned over and looked at the notebook. "The homing code!" he said. "That will take us right back to where this whole mess started, when Max reset the computer memory on Timebender!"

"If only we had seen this page sooner!" Allie said. She pressed the ALT and TAB keys at the same time.

"Look!" Toby shouted.

Grady and Allie looked out the windshield. There, hovering in front of the VW, was the Time Trooper vehicle.

"Not again!" Allie said. "Eight seconds to go!"

The doors of the hovercar opened up, the ramps came down, and the Time Troopers jumped out, pistol devices raised. "Time fugitives!" Trooper 7 said, approaching Allie's side of the car. "Surrender!"

Allie looked into the crystal lens of the pistol device—then covered her face with her hands. "Don't shoot!" she wailed.

Trooper 11 walked around to Grady's side and reached for the door handle—

And grabbed empty air.

The two Time Troopers looked at each other. Trooper 7 said, "They did it to us again!"

"Dude!" Toby said.

"Whoa!" Grady said.

Allie looked out the cracked windshield of Timebender. "Talk about your déjà vu—"

They were back in Max's backyard. And over there was Timebender, looking as shiny as new. And standing next to Timebender were—

Max, Allie, and Grady!

"We've got to warn them!" Allie said. She leaped out through the doorless driver's side. Grady jumped out the passenger side. Toby pushed his way from the backseat of the Volkswagen, tripped on his way out the door, and went sprawling onto the grass.

Allie, Grady, and Toby yelled warnings at Allie, Grady, and Max. They yelled, shouted, gestured—and none of it made any sense because they were all talking at once.

Suddenly, the air behind the battered Timebender shimmered. The shimmer became a strange black-and-white vehicle that floated above the ground. The Time Troopers had tracked them down.

"They found us!" Allie screamed.

"Let's get out of here!" Grady shouted.

"Aaaaggghhh!" Toby wailed.

They jumped back into the battered, flowered VW with the missing door. Allie took the driver's seat and immediately hit ESCAPE. Toby piled into the back, and Grady jumped into the passenger seat.

The Time Troopers came out of the hovercar, pistol

devices raised. "Halt!" Trooper 7 said. "Do not engage your time circuits!"

But even before the robot had finished speaking, Timebender was gone again. "This," said Trooper 7, "is getting to be a habit."

They were back in the time of the yellow sky, smoking volcanoes, and air that smelled like rotten eggs.

"Okay, Allie," Grady said. "We've got to get out of here fast. The Time Troopers are tracking us through time, so we need to stay a jump ahead of them."

"We need coordinates," Allie said. "If we keep entering random numbers, we'll just bounce around the fourth dimension like pinballs! Eventually, the batteries will be dead—and the Time Troopers will close in."

"But we don't know how to calculate the coordinates!" Grady said. "The only guy who can do that is Max!"

"God," Allie prayed, "we're in a real mess! Help!"

"Yes," Grady prayed, "please help us!"

"Will you dorks stop praying and *do* something?" Toby yelled.

"You might try these coordinates," said a voice from the backseat—a deep, rich, *golden* voice.

Grady and Allie turned around and their jaws dropped. Toby looked at the seat beside him—and screamed! An unearthly being sat beside Toby, robed in golden light.

"Gavriyel!" Grady and Allie shouted in unison.

The Emissary Gavriyel moved his finger through the air. Wherever his finger wrote, golden numbers floated. "Your friend, Max, asked me to locate you and send you to him. Simply enter these numbers, and Timebender will take you there." Gavriyel paused. "Oh, and you'd better work quickly. You have company."

They did, indeed. The Time Troopers had arrived again.

Allie read the glowing numbers, then tapped them into the keypad and hit ENTER.

The doors of the Time Troopers' hovercar swung open. The ramps swung down. The robots rushed out.

"Not enough time!" Grady said. "They'll get here before we timebend!"

"No, they won't," Gavriyel said with a glowing wave.

Instantly, both robots stumbled and fell flat on their metal faceplates.

"Well," Gavriyel said, "good-bye, Allie, Grady, and Toby. I'm glad I could help." Before the three time travelers could thank him, the Emissary was gone.

A second later, Timebender disappeared—leaving two frustrated robots behind.

@ @ @

Max McCrane and Laura Skyes sat on the curb at a little past one in the morning. A streetlight cast a cozy glow over them. Laura took something from her purse and held it out. "Here," she said. "This is yours."

The gold cross in Laura's hand sparkled in the light from the streetlamp.

"Thanks," Max said, "but I'd like you to have it." He reached out and closed Laura's fingers around the cross.

She looked at Max with shining eyes. "Thank you," she said. "I'll wear it always—and I'll remember," she said as she put on the cross.

There was a shimmer in the air, and a sigh on the breeze. Max and Laura looked at the street—

And Timebender appeared.

Max's mouth fell open. He stood up. "My car!" he said, astonished. The last time Max had seen Timebender, it had been shiny and new-looking. Now it was dented and crunched, the glass was broken, there was spray paint all over it, and the driver's-side door was gone. "What happened?"

Allie jumped out of the car, rushed to Max, and gave him a big hug. "Max!" Allie said. "I'm so glad to see you!"

"Allie!" Max said. "It's great to see you, too! But my car—"

Allie bit her lip. "I can explain—" But before Allie could say another word, Laura walked up to her and gave her a big hug.

"Allie!" Laura said. "I can't wait to tell you what happened!"

"Luna!" Allie said, backing away.

"Not Luna," Laura said. "From now on, call me Laura."

Allie looked at the smile on Laura's face, the gleam of joy in her eyes, the cross—and Allie knew it was true. The girl who stood in front of her had been reborn—a new person with a new name.

Grady came around the car and clapped Max on the back. "Max," he said, "you'll never believe what we've been through!"

"From the looks of things," Max said, "I think I'll believe it." Then he laughed. "But who cares about a busted car? The important thing is we're all together—and we're going home!"

"Dude!" Toby called from the backseat. "Let's go before those killer robots catch us again!"

Max looked at Allie and Grady. "Killer robots?"

Grady shrugged. "Long story—but Toby's right. We'd better go."

They all piled into the car. Allie and Laura squeezed into the back with Toby. Grady sat up front with Max. It took Max about thirty seconds to do the calculations. Then he entered the coordinates and pressed ENTER.

"Toby!" Allie said. "Will you stop scratching?"

"Dude! It itches!"

Timebender vanished in an orange shimmer.

A few more seconds passed.

Another shimmer appeared and took solid form. The Time Troopers had arrived too late again.

"We just missed them," Trooper 11 said, looking out the transparent bubble canopy.

"Well," Trooper 7 said, "we know where to find them—and this time we'll bring reinforcements."

◎ ◎ ◎

Timebender shimmered into existence in Max's backyard and everyone got out.

"Man!" Grady said. "It's good to be back!"

"Allie, Grady, Toby," Laura said, "tell us everything that happened to you!"

"Count me out!" Toby said, walking away.

"Toby!" Laura said. "What's your hurry?"

"Dude! I'm itching all over!" With that, Toby took off for home.

Allie turned to Max. "One thing I don't understand, Max," she said. "When we used the homing code to timebend back to our own time, and there were two Timebenders in your backyard—"

"Yeah?" said Max.

"The shiny Timebender was over here," Allie said, "and the beat-up Timebender was over there. I would have thought the homing code would have returned the beat-up Timebender to the same place as the shiny Timebender."

"It would have," Max said, "if I hadn't thought of all that when I programmed the homing code into the Timebender circuits. I added a little line of programming code to move the homing Timebender about twenty yards from the departure site. If two Timebenders ever tried to occupy the same space at the same time—*BOOM!*" He made an explosive gesture with his hands.

"How big a boom?" Allie asked.

"Well, I'm not certain of my calculations," Max said, "but I think it would probably vaporize everything in a radius of about half a light-year. That's, like, the whole solar system and then some. Good thing I thought of that, huh?"

"Yeah," Allie said. "A *real* good thing."

The air around the backyard shimmered. Moments later, black-and-white hovercars—a dozen of them—surrounded Max, Allie, Grady, and Laura. Max's backyard looked like a Time Troopers convention.

Laura gasped. "What's happening?"

The doors of a dozen hovercars swung open and the ramps of a dozen hovercars swung down. Twenty-four Time Troopers surrounded the human time travelers. Most of them had their crystal-lensed pistol devices pointed at Max, Allie, Grady, and Laura.

Time Trooper 7 stepped forward. "You will all surrender," it said. "We have you surrounded."

Max looked around at the Time Troopers and shrugged. "Okay," he said. "We surrender. What happens now?"

"You won't shoot us, will you?" Grady said.

"Shoot you?" Trooper 7 said.

"With those guns!" Grady said.

"What guns?" Trooper 7 asked.

Grady pointed to Trooper 7's pistol device.

Trooper 11 stepped forward and said, "The chrono-cams! You ran from us because you thought these were guns?"

"Chronocams!" Max said. "You mean—"

Trooper 7 held out its pistol device. "This chronocam is a three-dimensional camera we use to transmit images to Time Patrol Headquarters."

"We apologize for frightening you," Trooper 11 said.

"But," Trooper 7 said, "there is still the matter of your crime."

Allie gulped. "Our *crime?*"

"Yes," Trooper 7 said. The robot pointed to Max and Laura. "These two were not involved." It pointed to Allie and Grady. "But you two have violated the Temporal Security Act of 2099. There was another violator, a green-eyed boy with pink skin, but he seems to have escaped."

"Well," Allie said, "what is this Temporal Security Act of . . . whenever?"

"It is a law that forbids temporal trespassing," Trooper 7 said. "The years 2099 and beyond have been legally declared a no-time-travel zone. Time travelers are forbidden to enter. The penalties for violators are quite severe—up to a hundred years in prison."

Allie gasped. "But we didn't know!"

"Of course you didn't know," Trooper 7 said. "That's why all first offenders, like yourselves, are let off with a warning. If you had not run from us, we would have simply issued you a warning citation and let you return to your own time."

Grady slapped his forehead. "You mean this whole crazy chase we've been through was because we didn't stop and let you write us a warning?"

"Exactly," Trooper 7 said. A slot opened in the robot's belly and three slips of paper crawled out. The robot handed them to Grady and Allie. "The third one is for your fugitive friend—next time you see him."

"Well," Trooper 11 said, "we'll be going now." All around Max's backyard, Time Troopers got into their hovercars and disappeared in shimmer after shimmer.

"Good-bye, citizens," Trooper 7 said, then added, "Oh, and one more thing: Have a nice—"

"I know, I know," Allie said. "Traffic cops always give you a ticket then say, 'Have a nice day.'"

"We're Time Troopers," Trooper 7 said. "Our slogan is 'Have a nice forever.'"

Trooper 7 and Trooper 11 returned to their hovercar. Max, Allie, Grady, and Laura watched as a shimmer of light took the two robots out of their sight.

"'Have a nice forever,'" Laura Skyes said with a satisfied smile. "That's exactly what I'm going to do!"

More Timebender Adventures

Book 1: Battle Before Time

It was our first trip in Timebender, and we were lost. Then, just when I thought I had Timebender headed back to our time, we ended up somewhere before time—*in the middle of a full-scale war!* Planets were blowing up . . . weird lights were whirling all around us . . . we were running out of air . . . and there was no way back! That's when we met a strange new friend who changed our lives forever.

ISBN 1-4003-0039-8

Book 2: Doorway to Doom

An antique doorway . . . a bag of glow-in-the-dark eyeballs . . . and a mysterious intruder from the past. Who would've thought that such a strange combination could create a time transport that would pull me and my friends a thousand years into the past with no way back to our own time?

ISBN 1-4003-0040-1

Book 4: Lost in Cydonia

Toby Brubaker is in trouble—again. And he sees Timebender as the perfect getaway car . . . that is until he "overloads" my new antigravity device. Now Timebender's racing out of control and heading straight for Mars, setting off alarms at the International Space Station where a top-secret mission to the Red Planet is underway. (And I'd told my mom I was *only* going to take Grady, Allie, and her dad three feet up in the air to show them how it worked!)

ISBN 1-4003-0042-8